Go Love

a novel

Michael Gills

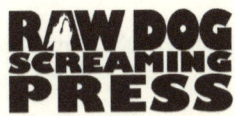

RAW DOG
SCREAMING
PRESS

Published by Raw Dog Screaming Press
Bowie, MD

First Edition

Cover photo by Nick Boren
Website: http://www.redbubble.com/people/nboren

Printed in the United States of America

ISBN: 978-1-935738-16-9

Library of Congress Control Number: 2011933280

www.RawDogScreaming.com

Other Books by Michael Gills

The Death of Bonnie and Clyde and Other Stories

Why I Lie: Stories

Acknowledgements

This story could not have been written without the love and support of Jill and Lyra Gills. I'd like to thank Captain Peter C. Peterson for his part in all this. Likewise, my gratitude goes to Ms. Patricia Buck–book lover and friend par excellence.

I'd like to thank the fine poet Gibbons Ruark and his wife Kay for their support and friendship over the years. The late great writers John Clellon Holmes and James Whitehead have a say here, as does Fred Chappell, who is very much with us. Jim Clark deserves high praise for his ongoing encouragement of a whole slew of us, as does François Camoin. For editing this novel in a rough form, I offer heartfelt thanks to Julianna Baggott. A mighty thank you goes out to Jennifer Barnes, my editor at Raw Dog Screaming Press. And this novel might not have seen the light of day if not for Eric Miles Williamson—literary kith and kin.

Finally, I'd like to thank Vicki and Larry Davis—*metakuye oyasin*.

Several of these chapters have appeared–in different forms–in the following publications for which grateful acknowledgment is given: chapter 1 as "Blue Run," *Verb Audioquarterly*, Vol. 2, Issue 2; chapter 9 as "When Up is Down," *Chattahoochee Review*, Summer 2006; chapter 14 as "How Jesus Comes," *McSweeney's 26*. Special thanks goes to Guy Lebeda and the Utah Arts Council for their continued support.

...For thou art with me here upon the banks
Of this fair river; thou my dearest Friend,
My dear, dear Friend; and in thy voice I catch
The language of my former heart...

from "Lines Composed A Few Miles Above Tintern Abbey,"
William Wordsworth

for Jacquelyn Treadwell Gills

I believe.

And for Ella, Edie, Peg, Jill and Lyra–
the fierce, beautiful women who bookend my life

Part One

1. June 14, 2002
Melbourne Beach, Florida

I'm knee deep in a blue run when Mama drowns in Arkansas. Gull, heron, stork dive the bait-slick water. Bluefish leap beyond the second breaker. For the quarter-mile school, I fish one rod. Each hit is violent, tight line whistling through the lips of waves. High tide rolls in. It's overcast. The wind is southwest. Even six ounces of pyramid lead swerves hard north. A surfer girl runs past, neon board looped to one ankle. She ducks under my line, hits the board hard on her tanned belly, paddles for the good waves. I'm very much alive. Be careful, I want to say, these murderous blues, they'll rip your head off, take a finger or a toe, it's happened. Fishing a good run brings on trance, the honest Zen of surfcasting the tide, horsing the lead and graphite with the eyelets swishing your ears. Dance into the water and let fly. The repetition—hours pass.

A Mexican family—I guess Mexican and I guess a family—works the surf a couple hundred yards up beach. They're having a time. These big-chested dark men, brilliant casters, catching Jesus out of the blues, giving them hell. The baitfish are in thick—menhaden, finger mullet, spot and croaker, they zing past. And these Latinos' wives or girlfriends or sisters stretch on colorful towels behind the coolers where sand sluices toward the dunes and signs say *Beware of Sea Turtles*—they're laying now. A mile-long stretch of public beach, you don't have to have a license and the man never checks your coolers. Two boys, fourteen, fifteen, romp beside the men's lines. They ride boogie boards and inflatables, brown skin against the green water.

The overcast sky starts to pinken. *Pink sky at night, sailor's delight*, that's what Renee always says. It's the sort of afternoon you can get your teeth into.

What I'm saying is that these people seem decent and hard working, like Stepwells and Harvells back home, and they have this Friday afternoon off like me to fish the rising tide within eyeshot of the millionaire beach palaces that line the coast toward Cocoa. We've hit the blue run square on the nose, and there's nothing save this labor, this motion, this way of being.

The Mexicans catch two-at-a-time on double rigs: tailor blues, three-pounders. We mirror each other this way for who knows how long. And I start thinking how right the world can be, how we're all knee-deep in this shit together. That's how blind I'm thinking, like the kid who grins into the jack-in-the-box that's about to knock his teeth out. It's an old story. The Mexicans see me too, cranking the blues, how I hang with them. Maybe they think I'm decent, or hardworking, and not one of the candy-ass tourists or snowbirds whose concrete driveways they pour, whose houses they roof and whose yards they mow and whose bugs they poison in the ungodly heat. Whatever, workers move my heart. My people are workers. I choose to see them as workers this afternoon. This is how I'll remember them. These workers and me, we watch each other land fish as the boys surf riptides.

How much time passes this way? Baiting and casting, reeling the torpedo blues onto shore, the bright gills and darting eyes. His teeth will lay you open. The smell of fish, oily and sweet. When he hits, let drag go, let him run and jump and feel the hook buried in his jaw. Keep the rod tip high, throw your head back and scream *come home to Daddy* like my writer-friend Ray Ray out on the outer banks drunk under the Orionid meteor shower. Use the wave, break the run, goddamnit, bring him home. Up onto the sand. Grab his pale blue shoulders and lean into his face. Let the hemostats sway from your neck down to his mouth. Get a grip on the hook's snell, twist it from his mouth. Cut his throat. Lay him bleed with his kith and kin, under bloody ice and beer and heads-on shrimp. Smear blood on your ball cap so you'll remember this day, even when it morphs into the day it will become. Rebait, cast a hunk skyward—let fly. *Be.*

Maybe it's after five when the blitz slows. The length of my white rod, the eleven-footer glistens with scales and blood and my arms are spattered to the elbows. I've promised Cap, Renee's father, I'll cook tonight, make fish tacos and frijoles negras, salsa and corn tortillas. My word's good.

I'm forty goddamn years old: why not piss in the ocean, swim out and get my hair wet, wash the blood and guts off my body? A shadow slides through the trough when I enter. The Atlantic is cold water, best to dive through the incoming wave, split the lip, that's what I do, with the blues and screaming birds thinning now, the run played out. Over the second bar, in the wake of the blue run, I give to the current and don't know about Mama, how it goes for her now. We breathe goodbye, her mind flashing the way the sun does when it goes down on open sea. The feast is set, food for the table, good meat from the open water between worlds. What is there to know for certain about anything?

This strand is world famous for its riptide. The undertow here drowns the best swimmers, hauling them along the ocean floor, turning them under the waves. I've felt the pull, and it's a bastard today, the gravity of open ocean. *Peligro*, the signs say, *Danger, Beware*. Watch your ass. Drawings show these hilarious stick figures drowning, blue zig-zags pulling them under. People are always getting sucked under and spat back up, sometimes breathing sometimes not. On stray dunes, crosses are decorated with plastic flowers to mark drownings. But if you're strong and have the patience to ride the thing out, just hold your breath until it spits you up, then you can make it, that's what I believe. With a little luck and patience, you can ride out a rip.

Sharks are another story. They'll come at you from behind and attack in rounds, and once you're hit, Katy bar the door. Melbourne Beach surfers have rituals for sharks, like never ever eating their flesh or calling them shitheads, or generally speaking ill of their presence within sight of ocean. Rocky and Bet, Renee's brother and sister-in-law, have dances and necklaces and shark mantras. They beat drums, light and jump through hoola-hoops soaked with gasoline. Oh hell, sharks, I'm thinking sharks and let saltwater sluice through my mouth. They've never bothered me. I body surf a wave into a late afternoon after fishing the blue run, clean now, all the blood washed away.

When I get out, the bull-chested men charge me, full-sprint, throwing sand in little puffs. *Son-of- a-whore*, one yells. The other's face is white, his lips moving.

He's making damn good time. The boys haul ass as well, at me—and what've I done in this world? To get charged out of the clear blue? That's how it seems, standing there with water dripping off my balls.

They're good runners, screaming *higo de punta*—full of piss and vinegar and conviction. A good sprinter can do a hundred meters in eleven seconds, add a few ticks for the sand. It can be a long time—much time for thinking, hearing your own heart beat in the vacuum of middle ear. Believe me. I've run the 100 enough to know. The spring of the big tornado, we'd travel to Stuttgart or Tupelo or Lonoke Jackrabbit Relays, with buckets of chicken and dirty sanitary socks stretched up over our calves, with jaguar running spikes and red batons and pole vault poles and shiny starting blocks. The air smelled of Kramergesic the trainers rubbed into our thighs and calves, while honey-breathed cheerleaders thrust hips over the green infield. *Are you satisfied? Are you satisfied?* they chanted. Pistol fire announced false starts, twin repeats echoing between the home and visitor-side bleachers, and the asphalt was spongy and burned my knees in the on-your-mark position in lane three, and the man said, *get set* and the sun shone on our spikes and the gun was finally fired for real. I'd come out low and burn the first forty, then rise and pump the sprint in-between. In Lonoke County, with boatloads of time to think about who I was and where I was going, and what kind I'd come from. And this one time, I swear to god, at the Jackrabbit Relays, in heat two of the hundred, a guy named Bobby Cox—somehow his dick got out of his jock strap about fifty yards into the race he was winning, just flopped out of his jock strap and bounced to beat the band. Everybody got quiet and he just kept on running, through the pink finish ribbon and out of the stadium, out into Honeysuckle Lane, he just kept on running and he's still out there running. So runners, I'm trying to say, they're thinkers, and what these Mexicans are thinking, the sand coming up from their feet in white whiffs, is beyond me, a genuine mystery about to happen.

I draw the knife from my belt scabbard, square feet and face them straight on. Which must look pretty funny to them, this white dude with a piddly four-inch blade.

Next proves how Stepwell I am to the core, how the great blind spot unites us. The men, brothers I can tell after they pass, pay me no mind. The boys run right on past as well, not even a nod at my knife or a *son of a whore*. The sand squeaks beneath my feet. Not twenty yards away, just at the point where I, myself, Joey Stepwell Harvell just crawled on hands-and-knees out of the surf, a sea turtle struggles.

A goddamn sea turtle, big as a buffalo.

They nest in dunes between the ocean and highway, and signs warn of heavy fines for anyone who fucks with their doings. It grunts and belches and hisses through its beak, makes six-inch thrusts up toward the dunes that it won't make by nightfall. And this with the Mexicans giving it all kinds of hell. They dance circles, rapping its briny shell, singing *son of a whore, son of a whore, son of a whore* which sounds holy out of their mouths, like some miracle is going on this second. The women sashay by and I think to say something in Spanish. And still, this sea turtle puts out such an effort as to astound us for a good thirty minutes as the sun gets low and my mama's lovely brown eyes see something I've never seen. The boys push her from behind, and the men get their whole shoulders into her. The bull-chested brothers lift and push the shell and this helps, though it's all out illegal, sure as shit. I join in, help, put my shoulder to the task, though I know—don't fuck with a turtle.

The pretty women, maybe the boys' mothers, offer soft words to encourage us, to give us strength, or that's how it sounds, like they urge us and this sister turtle toward a nest where she can lie in peace as the sand cools and the day fades and the stars come out, and the sand crabs walk sideways. Lie awhile before the easy trip down to low tide. Reenter the ancestral waters. Swim home, sister.

That's how I'll remember the afternoon. Me and the Mexicans. The olive-skinned women with love on their voices, the blues and the lard-ass turtle, some pink in the sky, sand in white whiffs. Soft voices.

I dig in, hoist my shoulders into her, help the men lift as the boys push and the women chant. No one sees us, the seven of us grunting with this five-hundred-pound turtle. We make a dune just before sunset. The Mexicans hug and kiss each other, make crosses over their chests then turn and walk up the beach. They pack their gear and walk away from my life forever. Something huge has cut the line on my eleven-footer, a blue, shark maybe, whatever— the line's cut clean. I imagine what's left of the rig being dragged across the bottom where riptides roll. A heron's made off with a few blues from my cooler, but there's cold beer and the night coming, with fish cleaning and tacos, Cap's sea stories and his wife, Meg, the merry matriarch of the family whose hazel eyes shine down through the generations. Renee and my daughter Lara are poolside. We'll spend this night between river and ocean; within earshot, the waters will break and break.

The phone call comes after midnight.

The whir of Cap's lawn sprinklers outside in the dark. Between the ocean and river—that Florida taste in the air when every living thing grows violently. By morning, newly deformed hedges will assault you alongside the oleanders. All that happens while we sleep in bedrooms with their ceiling fans that sometimes creak rhythmically or issue slight cries.

Renee shakes me. O.W., my stepfather, is on the phone.

Lights are on through the doorway and out into the house.

A cold receiver is pressed into my jaw. The digital clock says twelve something. An instant passes when it's still possible to walk away, to hang up, walk up the street and jump in the ocean, let the tide do what it will.

"Joey?"

"O.W.?"

"I got bad news. Mama's gone home."

"*Home?*"

Renee whispers *no*.

"She died this afternoon. Drowned. Of a heart attack."

Renee intuits. Her sob is a moan, one mournful note. Like a dove. I sit on a bed beside a window near the ocean, the cold phone against my face. My wife's beside me. One mournful note. I hear Cap's feet swish away over the big tile floor.

"Mama drowned of a heart attack?"

"Yeah."

"What?"

His voice is wrong. Once when I was a kid, he kicked his way into Mama's bedroom and she screamed for me to get help, that he was killing her. I picture him big as a barn, sitting at the glass kitchen table piled with her medical bills, maybe a stray love letter from that California flake. The television's on, I can hear it, taped golf. The players set their mouths, swing sand wedges.

"She drowned in her hot tub. From a heart attack. I tried to call her from Rocky Mount but nobody answered. I've always dreaded that." His voice is high and strange, like a preacher trying to cry. "Traceleen found her."

"How'd you know I was here?"

"She wrote it down," he says.

"O.W.?"

"I'm locking the house up till tomorrow."

"O.W.?"

"I'll talk to you then."

The dial tone is hard to talk about—it gets into your teeth, under your fillings, like cicadas in August when all the run over dogs have bloated and people hang water moccasins from tree limbs for the rain that won't come.

"Mama's gone home." I hear myself tell Renee the absurd news.

By the sound of the birds, the new day is going down outside where it's still Florida. Up the coast, Cape Kennedy, where men defied gravity to take the fat moon. Further north, Saint Augustine, legendary fountain of youth. Ponce de Leon sipped of these waters after the Indian slaughters. Water, always water, the river on one side and the ocean on the other, the entirety of the state surrounded.

2. Josephine

I've been drowning my whole life. Mistake number one, Buddy Washer, got busted dressed as Santa Claus on a border bus near Nogales, his belly stuffed with an eigh- pound brick of weed, just what Joey weighed at birth, eight pounds even. I'd met Buddy in Little Rock when I was nineteen and blind as white bread and crazy to get out of Arkansas—him showing those pretty teeth and swept back hair and movie star tan. His voice was different. He wasn't southern for one thing, and he could lie his way up one side of your heart and down the other—not that a southern man won't do that too, in spades. His people, back in Arizona, held seats in the State Legislature. They ran this huge old family ranch near Tombstone, where his great, great grandfather, Johnny Tremain, put all the outlaws under Boothill Cemetery dirt a hundred years ago. They ran Appaloosas and Quarterhorses, held big family cookouts every Sunday out under the turquoise sky where cactus bloomed and the desert paintbrush shone like fire in spring time when the rains came.

Theirs was one of the oldest families in Tucson and the spread near Tombstone had been in the family since the days when Geronimo forayed down to escape the *federalies* and the bounty on his head. Buddy told a story of how his great grandmother, Katy, was just a girl when the medicine man showed up with a band of ragged braves, camped a night on the ranch, just outside the fenceline. Katy, her brother and her sisters, had hidden an entire night inside the fireplace chimney. Next morning, the Indians were gone, vanished. Geronimo ended up signing his name for quarters at the World's Fair in Seattle. Why I know all this, I don't know, but on a frosty night, Geronimo fell drunk out of a wagon and froze to death in an Oklahoma ditch. All he ever wanted was to go home. Geronimo—World War II paratroopers shouted *Geronimo!* when they stepped out into sky.

That's me, say *Geronimo*! and jump.

Buddy was like that. He got us married by a sleepy justice somewhere in the big heart of Texas, then talked all night. The radio cackled just beneath the story of his first wife, how she'd had a little baby girl then got killed by a semi-truck. The grief-sick daughter had up and quit talking, hadn't said a word since its mama died. Driving between Clovis and Tucumcari, while Buddy slept and this huge land got light again, I pictured *her*, how I'd hold her to me and say her name and be her mama and she'd be whole again. By Las Cruces, I'd remade myself into the mother of all lonely children, and the whole wild west brightened before me.

We rolled into south Tucson in April, the month when dogwood blooms in Arkansas, and everything Buddy Washer ever told me was a lie. The Washer family spread was three rusty trailers that sat out of level on a bare dirt lot by a Dairy Queen where donors from the Plasma Center slept off wine drunks with vomit on their shirts and dark circles where they'd peed their pants. Buddy's car overheated. When we drove onto the oil-stained dirt, the yard beside one of the trailers, a dwarf hopped out wolf-whistling, just like that, like this was the way all Washers came home. He dragged a water hose from a fence line spigot, popped the hood and sprayed the radiator. It bubbled and hissed until Buddy tied a towel around one hand and unscrewed the cap. Overflow spurted up over our heads onto the trailer roof, so that the whole bunch of them stepped through the busted out screen, like walking through a blank space with their dogs to welcome me home. Buddy's mom, Violet, stared me through. I was two months pregnant with Joey already, and—honest—it felt like she was seeing my baby straight through me.

They threw a party that first night. One of the brothers walked over to a liquor store and came back with a quart of tequila dangling from either arm, a shriveled up lime in his pocket and a carton of Marlboros. The men—Buddy and his brothers, and maybe one of the resurrected plasma drunks—cooked, roasting meat over charcoal in a foil-lined hole in the dirt. Somebody'd drug out half a goat or lamb—Jesus I hope goat or lamb—though it was probably dog. I'm sure now, dog. A mutt. So they cooked this great big side of what they said was goat or lamb—but was really dog—over charcoal and drank tequila and smoked Marlboros while the sisters and Grandma Violet asked me everything from my shoe size to whether or not I'd been a virgin before Buddy and I did it. The radio was loud—a Spanish station rolling the *Rs*—and all of them smoked and kept offering their packs to me until I started saying *yes* and took a cigarette and a few tequilas.

They asked about my people, what religion we were and if anybody had any money, which they didn't, until in came a roasting pan full of dog that I told myself was goat or lamb. Give it to them, it tasted good with black beans and charred corn and all these salsas. A brother, taller and heavier than Buddy, started dancing with one of the sisters. The godawful dogs barked outside. One of the boys asked me to dance and I did, and we drank tequila and they spoke Spanish—Buddy's big pretty smile bright now.

"See? I told you you'd love us. And we'd love you. We're rich," he said and hugged me to his chest. Buddy Washer kissed me. "We're all rich," he sang out. And we danced and sang and smoked Marlboros and ate dog or goat or lamb burritos until the lights got turned out and we slept wherever we fell.

Rich, my ass. I woke hungover to cigarette butts and spilt tequila, flies buzzing, dirty dishes stacked in the sink. And that wasn't even the worst. Nor the cat licking the sink faucet or the shock of understanding that these people breathing out the sides of their mouths on the floor were now my people from here on out, no matter what, our blood was mixed in my womb. And that wasn't even the kicker, there was more. Outside looked like yesterday and tomorrow. Like I suffered from love at first sight, only in reverse—I'm sure some dopehead shrink's thought up a name for that way of being, how I found myself that morning. But even that, the letdown, knowing how I'd been fished all along. That wasn't the worst of it, not by a long shot.

Buddy'd slept on the broken recliner. Even like that, pants unzipped and flies on his ears, he wasn't so bad, not at all loathsome. A natural liar—he made everything seem possible—all you needed was to believe. *Believe in me*, he'd say, and I believed in him. That was April 1960—I was two months pregnant with Joey, full of hope and life and the promise of going west to the land of dreamy dreams, all that crock. So all this uncouthness I'd brought on myself, and my unborn child, I'd just have to work around it, nearly anybody can do that, can't they? My daddy always said, you want to see somebody's colors, catch'em down— see how they go about living the day when all hell's broken loose. Anybody can be good when life is sweet, he said, knocking pipe fire out on the prosthesis that was his right leg, painted flesh-colored. And then he'd say something like, "the higher you climb, the more of your ass shows," so who knows about him. Who can tell me a thing about any man? Anyway, I knew that I could deal with Buddy and his family, and I'd only seen a sliver of the place. Maybe I got the whole place backwards up front. Mount Lemon, the peak Buddy'd pointed out through his car's steamy windshield, gleamed in the distance. Snow was up there, a shock, given this heat. Everything was possible. If snow could stay put above a hellacious desert, wasn't anything at all possible?

"Where's the little girl, Buddy? Who quit talking?"

My husband opened one blue-green eye, then the other. He rubbed flies off his ears and smiled. His teeth were even and perfect, even my mother had been amazed by Buddy's teeth, not a filling in his head, not a gap, no visible decay. "Who?"

Vi got up off the couch, turned the television on and lit a cigarette. The rest of the brothers and sisters lay on the floor, with dogs and each other.

"Your girl. Her mama died in a car wreck."

I couldn't understand a word coming out of the TV. My stomach growled. The air went a little hazy with Vi's smoke. All during the night ride, after the sleepy justice married us, my newlywed husband went on about the wife who'd died in a wreck, and the girl who hadn't spoken a word since her mother's death. He'd told me the doctors claimed she'd never recover, not without a new mommy—a new mother's love.

"Where is she?"

Vi shook her head at the idiot on television and one sister propped on an elbow, looking from Buddy to me to Vi and back. Davey strutted in and whistled at the sight of us. "Lord," he said. "What did one pissant say to the other pissant?"

The world can be a quiet, quiet place. If you're a pregnant fool in Arizona, this earth can spin through silence such as has never been heard.

"Sure beats the piss out of me," Davey said.

Vi laughed and so did the sister leaning on an elbow. Buddy threw both hands up and let them fall to the bare chair arms and shut his eyes again. And that was that—they just went on and let the day unwind as if nothing had happened, as if it was good common sense to have your stories straight in matters of love and death.

Vi stared through my flesh, my baby—*Joey?*

My mother says the blue-gowned doctors at Pima County Regional walked out and said, "The mother won't make it," and then, "The baby won't make it," and then "We'll lose them both," all Christmas Day long, 1960. Carolers sang "Silent Night" up and down ammonia-scented corridors, all through the pediatric unit O.R. When labor started I'd been standing in the kitchen of the bungalow we'd rented, lighting candles on one of those angel mobiles—the three that spin clockwise with gold wings, dinging. And the pains came just as the bells started ringing. The house was quiet. Dee'd gone out for a walk, disgusted with the place, having spent Christmas Eve with Buddy's people. Violet had coughed up brown phlegm and kept spitting it in a sock she kept in the palm of her left hand, all through Christmas Eve dinner. Dwarf Davey's little Chihuahua bared its teeth and growled all through pie time.

Tiny bells dinged and I looked out the window. Way off, a thirty foot saguaro waved, like a dark man telling me to come home: behind him, a white cloud pierced the blue sky. Christmas morning, the pains came. We'd decorated an avocado tree with a tin foil angel and strings of cranberries and popcorn. Dee'd brought a branch of Arkansas cedar, set it up on the cracked fireplace mantle and burned some, so the house smelled like home. Surely it was a good sign, Christmas, my baby coming on Christmas. The cedar smell made me think of my daddy, how I wished he'd walk in the front door, just come on in singing "I'm Ding-Dong-Daddy from Dumas" and knocking pipe fire out on his wooden leg, a little pipe-circle on the flesh-colored paint. I was homesick when the pains hit, Christmas Day in Arizona.

I wrote: *dear mama, the baby's coming now. it could be worse, we could be in Las Vegas with a roomful of those little growling dogs. vi could be there with her sock. merry christmas. i love you with all of my heart, your daughter, Josephine.*

My water broke in the driver's seat of Dee's Buick, right out in the hospital parking lot. I leaked down the long concrete sidewalk under that gigantic sky, sweating and dizzy. The long concrete sidewalk to EMERGENCY. And I remember the water mixed with blood leaking down my leg and somebody helping me when the real pain hit, and being embarrassed at being seen like that. The big doors swung open and shut and then time just kind of stopped, froze, just like now. Not being entirely conscious has its benefits. I can see that day so clearly. Dee says they called in a pot-bellied preacher who kept saying *Time?*

I awoke to carolers singing *silent night, holy night, all is calm, all is bright*, then that hilarious round yon virgin part. For all my life, I've never understood the *round yon virgin* part—a man wrote that, surely to god. Dee was holding both my hands, her sweet gardenia smell. She kept saying, "It's okay baby, it's okay baby," and crying a little, and it dawned on me that I *was* her baby. *Sleep in heavenly peace* somebody's voice sang and Dee said, "Baby, it's okay," and I got this bad feeling that my baby'd died, so I started screaming *no!* from some deep down place I'd forgotten about. That's when I felt the stitches rip, just open up, so it felt like I was pouring out of myself, and somebody sang *holy infant so tender and mild*. There's this blank place where everything's already happened, where your dreams are the dreams of grieving people, the way the bereaved feel guilty. They keep driving past the house where the dead person once lived, slowing down to look through the windows or stopping to take a clipping from the forsythia bush. Remembering Christmas and Thanksgiving and Easter, how the cars drive by outside, how you can feel people looking in and thinking about you. I can feel his eyes looking through the window, taking a branch from my forsythia, feeling me there, saying he's sorry, saying I'm his baby, saying he loves me, saying *forgive me*.

Then I woke up. "Where's my baby?"

"Your boy," I was told, and it was a jolt because I didn't know what came next. Dwarf or legless—anything's possible. "He's being brought to you by nurse Cindy. Don't eat solids for a while. Not till the meds wear off. There will be considerable pain. Think of it as good hurt—all your nerves functioning. Am I saying too much?"

"Where's my baby?"

"You'll love your child in time." The woman's green eyes regarded me through thick glasses.

"I want my baby."

"There could be a desire to hurt the child," she said. "This is normal. Pay attention to your moods, write them down, keep a record."

My body didn't feel like my body at all. Nothing, just a dull thereness, and I remembered how Daddy'd get phantom charley horses in his missing leg after the accident, how he'd cry and get crazy and we'd have to massage just the right spot on his stump.

"*Right now*," I said.

The ICU door opened and in walked a tar-headed woman who laid Joey right on my chest. I'd never be alone again. The moment I saw his face, I knew it. I'd never be alone again.

"He looks like my daddy."

3. Joey

The sun is out, very fierce, Saturday, July 15 and I am unprepared. Today's schedule has been set for weeks. Rocky and Bet, Renee's brother and sister-in-law have adopted a Guatemalan toddler and today is *You Are Invited to a Beach Baby Shower* day. They've planned beer and barbecue at a pavilion reserved down island on the ocean side. Mama'd never in her life fuck up a baby shower—it just wasn't in her blood. Sprinklers click on in the back yard. I smell coffee.

In the bathroom mirror, my face—her eyes and widow's peak, I don't know the rest. I put on shorts and one of Cap's ball caps. Renee looks shaken when I finally walk in; she stares at the floor, what a lot of people do, I'll learn, when they learn your mother's just died.

Cap says, "Morning, Joey. I'm sorry, son."

Meg frowns deeply. She says, "There's Danish on the island."

"What's wrong daddio?" Lara hugs me, her face tanned from three days in the sun.

My daughter's been sleeping on a foldout couch with stuffed teddy bears. Cap's naval officer sword hangs above the closed closet and a folded up Destroyer flag is framed beside a picture of teenage Renee with sleek hair and a pouty face. His desk is a jumble, letters from Senators and subscription bills from Horny Housewives and a picture of Rocky, shirtless on some Costa Rican mountainside. He looks like Meg.

Lara turns my face to hers with her little hand. "Why do you stay in bed so long, Daddy?"

"Mama died yesterday." It just comes out.

Lara says, "Died?"

"Went home."

She nods so I see her thinking. "Oh," she says.

We're all at the long glass-covered table that looks out onto the kidney shaped pool with its tile mosaic turtles and little statue of Saint Francis of Assisi. Lara's humming this song about three elephants. Squirrels tightrope the telephone wire beyond the pool. Renee passes a sheet of paper she's downloaded with airfare prices—out of this world.

"Take the rental," Cap says. "Steal the son of a bitch."

He's fried a plateful of sausages and is going to town on eggs three ways— sunny side for Meg, scrambled for Lara and Renee, over-easy for me, a skillet of hashbrowns popping on one back burner. "That's what I'd do."

Meg says, "Today's the shower." Her hands tremble and a quiver sets in at the corners of her lips. Renee has a framed black and white of her as a bride, dragging this long white train, so beautiful and strange. She'd once left a diary on our night stand. Inside was written, top ten disappointments of my life. *I'll never have a daughter who's a beauty queen*, one entry reads. Another says, *How can she love him?*

"Just take the truck. Drive it on out. Turn it in in Little Rock. What can they do?"

O.W. and Traceleen were just now deciding on the bride-white casket, the shining Deluxe model with silver-plated hardware, the most expensive unit in Arkansas, maybe, because Mama's come into all that insurance money that's freed up now. A ceremony's being planned with Brother Dellwood Walker in Lonoke First Baptist. Appropriate verses are being chosen. Her will has been opened, the one she's kept under the black address book on her night stand. The funeral home has been notified. My tomato plants blister under the Utah sun. The obituary has begun.

I say, "I'm sorry this has happened."

Meg says, "Don't."

"I'm sorry. We have to go home to Mama's goddamn wedding."

She turns her eyes up to me—the same hazel with the yellow flecks my daughter sees me through. Meg shakes her head and gazes at me as if I've breathed fire. "You said wedding."

True. In my head, the mix-up's begun.

Baby Luis' shower is full-swing by the time we park outside the beach pavilion, beside a rusted Toyota pickup with a bumper sticker that says *War Is For People*

Who Don't Fish. Rocky and Bet spot us right off, start looking at the ground and make a point of trying to stop having a good time for a while. Bet's mother is in from Texas—she shares the same birthday as Cap, so it's been kind of a double party that Mama's crashed. Thelma holds baby Luis on one shoulder, the green Atlantic spreading out behind her back, where some of Rocky's hippy friends who haven't gone Republican yet throw horseshoes and sip Coronas. Thelma flew half a steer out from her Texas ranch, so the air's dense with grill smoke. It's hot and party-goers shake our hands and look at the ground like they just said hello to the shadow of death, except for Lara, who draws a crowd.

Renee drifts. She goes to her brother and the big table overflowing with gifts wrapped in surfboard-print paper. Everybody wears a bikini or tank top. A boatload are buzzed already, a couple flying these big careening kites into neighboring cabana roofs and the beach between dune grass and surf. Bet's a born again, right-wing, ex-college-surfer girl, shrimper, army corps of engineer dope-smoker who loves to fight and talk Jesus. She's got that glint in her eyes. She once argued a man to death. At a family reunion, she just kept at him till the poor bastard had a heart attack and died on the sand. She sips Corona—*mas fina cerveza*—flashes teeth at me, and talks to *Anti-girl*, the Republican groupie FIT secretary who's managed to get her claws into one of Rocky's Marine Biologist Engineer buddies. A looker, now she's with a pharmaceutical company, in charge of wining and dining doctors, pitching all the new anti-depressants, so she calls herself the *Anti-girl*, matches mini-skirts to her dirt-colored eyes, only now she's pregnant and looks real sick. I have the urge to walk out past the second sand bar, out to the weedline and beyond, get swallowed by sea and shark, let the rip tumble me where it will. The smell of cooked fat pours over us.

I know I'll die now. Hell, maybe Lara'll take the call after midnight, isn't that how it happens? The phone rings in the dark. Laughter on the answering machine's breath. I've read that everything that humans find funny—especially ducks and predicaments involving the number three or K sounds or anything resembling the sound of a fart—arises from the knowledge that we will die. The famously fat poet writes about how the undertaker sewed bits of plastic into his mother's gums, so she grinned at you from her casket.

During the viewing everybody could tell that she was happy with Jesus and the holy ghost in heaven.

The one authentic redneck here, a Jacksonville native in yellow Bermuda shorts, hands me a can of Pabst and asks if I ever got sober after that last charter trip. I met him during the three-day debauch that was Bet and Rocky's wedding, when we all got beer buzzed on the head boat Cap chartered, fishing all day for grouper out on Twenty Mile Reef. That night I accompanied the groomsmen to Tootsie's Nightlife, where aerobic beach queens lapdanced one and all and I got too drunk to sign the bill, so Mark scribbled my name for me.

"Can you rephrase the question?"

"You been fishing?"

"A little. You?"

"We're pregnant. I fish every goddamn chance come around."

"Good for you."

"Yeah," Mark says. He looks up from the dirt into my eyes. "I'm real sorry."

"Does everyone know?"

"Yeah. Rock told us."

The crowd visibly straightens when Cap and Meg cruise in, the Ford Explorer's windshield covered with plastic decals that make guards go into triple salute conniptions whenever he drives into Patrick Air Force Base to stock up on vodka and Prozac.

Meg's socks are bright white, cuffed over the ankle. She puts on her people face and works her way to the gift table where Renee and I've wrapped up a baby backpack with a fifth of Stolichnaya tucked in the pouch. Cap shakes my hand and looks me in the face. It's hard to say how he feels, but I know he means it, that he's had to tell many, many men, out on those destroyers in gray seas, that their mothers have passed away, their wives have left them for their best friends. His own mother died of cancer—no piece of cake, saying the long goodbye. Anyway, I register this and feel comfort, and that's when *Anti-girl* gets nauseated and starts to vomit right up on all the gifts, so that somebody screams and people clear a big circle. Meg glares, and I see her catch herself—all those iffy moments entertaining dingbat officer's wives, all that training, she recovers in an instant. Cap never even sees.

I'm here. I've managed that much, and I haven't been shitty to anybody, that much I've achieved. All's well with the *Anti-girl* now, and Meg's going on with Thelma about baby Luis. Renee is immersed entirely with her brother in the old promise to buy back the family farm house up in New Jersey. It's a day from an otherworld dream, where everything has already happened and it's okay to let your breath out for a second, sip beer, look at the water and be. Just *be*. The new you— the *you* you are now. Summer, June, the month of weddings, and in that other world you're best man in Dee's makeshift wedding for O.W. and Mama, on the thirteenth floor of the Himalaya House apartment, the elevator door just opening to the mirrored hall and it's thirty-five years ago. Me and O.W. wear spit-shined shoes and matching suits and clip-on ties. The apartment windows are open. And it's a bright day, let me tell you, Mama is so happy. She keeps dabbing the corners of her eyes with lace gloves. We'll have our own house with a swing and slide soon, and I can set up a tent and sleep in the backyard all night if I like. My brother Jimmy, he's on the way. Mama's wedding day, she wears white chiffon. Her black hair is tied back—I see her widow's peak. She's lithe and smells of gardenia; maybe this is when it starts to get all mixed-up in my head.

I'm best man.

"Joey, sweety," Mama says, "I love you with all my heart," and maybe this is the exact split-second when I get it backwards in my head. I'm standing in front of the preacher in a shirt and tie, dressed just like O.W. Mama's taken care of that. There I am standing between them, the three of us face to face with this double-chinned man of God who possesses the power to conjoin a woman to a man till death do them part. I'm standing there between them when he says, "In the sight of Almighty God, will you take this woman to be your wife?"

What did I know about men? I'd never met my blood father, never smelled him after he'd mowed the grass, which probably never even happened in bullshit Arizona. I'd never seen my mother kiss a man on the mouth. I'd first learned about my wacky lineage on a night when thunder scared me to her bed. I was born on Christmas Day and we both almost died—her water had broken. She hemorrhaged and the priest was summoned; we'd both die, a masked physician told the family. I knew that later, I'd somehow been her confidant and protector, and that having me around had helped her through hard times. We were lucky to have had each other, me and Mama. I knew we'd somehow been in danger out West, and that she'd risked a lot to get us out. And from sitting in Grandpa Stepwell's duck boat listening to her and Ruby talk for what seemed like hours once, I knew that my blood father had tried to kill her, for real. Marrying O.W. was related to all that, this much I knew, this much made sense.

"I'll take her," I'm saying. "To have and to hold."

The preacher grins at O.W. and Grandmother Dee says, *Joey*. But O.W. doesn't smile. Neither does Mama. They know I mean it. Standing there between them in spit-shined shoes, I keep saying it—*I'll take her, I'll take her* until the hand comes over my mouth.

Out under the sun, a quiet moment, Rocky's holding Baby Luis up for all the world to see. A descendent of Mayans, the Guatemalan baby's flint-black hair whips in the wind. Tears shine in the adoptive father's eyes. He holds the boy up in the bright sunshine, throws his head back and hollers, "Here's to swimmin' with bowlegged women." He says, "May your life be a good one, Luis." Bet joins him, mother, son, father. Beyond us is blue water—I sense Mama, this is her to the core.

"Hooray," somebody says, "To a good life."

"Here, here!" Cap shouts.

4. Josephine

For a long time I didn't tell Joey about his daddy, though the thought never left me alone, not with the way his hair waved back over his forehead and those green-blue eyes, and the way he held himself, even when he was just a little boy and I'd see him peddling the yellow tricycle. I'd see the handlebar streamers and he'd smile at me and it would break my heart all over again. Dee went easy on me with Joey around, an angel, first grandson right there in her own apartment. For a while, we had peace.

Buddy threatened to drive out and take Joey back. And that's exactly what he tried—once. I stayed home days then, and what else was there to do? Joey's got this tangential imagination, he was never bored, never without this strong link to some other world or plane or something. That's how it seemed. He was never a problem, but the boredom, the tedium, the sitting in the hot, hot front room that always smelled like burned coffee and pinto beans, all those sad, silly soap operas.

I started painting birds.

A few weeks into July, I talked Dee into buying a short list from the art supply store: water colors, three brushes, charcoal and stump paper, a putty eraser, some colored pencils and an X-Acto knife. She found one of those big folding sketch pads full of the kind of paper that can take a beating and I was set. So Joey and I moved our days out into the front yard, a small corner lot beside Thayer Street, which the lispy neighbor called *Prayer Street*, which it sort of was, if drawing your son into a bird can be thought of as prayer. The yard was on the apartment building's front side, a square of Bermuda where dog walkers did business. Dee believed it was a good sign when neighbors walked their dogs, way better than Scranton—her old home place, where hillfolk let their mutts run wild in the heat and perfectly sane people fished for chickens off front porches when the purple hull peas were hulled. Little Rock was, Dee'd say, the *Capitol.* She was number three auditor for the Department of Finance and spent days driving her Toyota to Paragould and Rison and Dirty Devil, checking city ledgers and school district funds, keeping the country people straight. Lord save your soul if you screwed up. With Dee you'll find your butt up river, picking peas on the County Farm.

Buddy came as a postman.

This was July bleeding to August, when the heat finally wins out and people move around stunned, half out of their minds. Joey'd invented a game that day of walking a spiral from the inside out, squatting on chubby legs and staring at the Bermuda grass as if there lay the answer to all things. I'd just lined out a rough of his face as an owl, how his nose hooked like my daddy's, the high forehead and widow's peak. A strong chin. Blue eyes with the Stepwell glint inside them. He'd take a punch some day. And he'd be wild in love just like the rest of us.

It's not like we were under the witness protection program. Finding us couldn't have been too much trouble, though casing us, inventing the Postman malarkey, and probably having his escape planned to a T, that's Buddy. I should have been on the lookout, but I wasn't, and neither was Dee, which surprises me now that I reconsider. He'd likely tromped past me and Joey a dozen times already, stuffing the apartment mailboxes with grocery ads and letters soon to be returned to sender with big red question marks magic markered through the fake people residing at fake addresses. No stamps, even. Maybe Buddy'd come close to doing it a few times, laying hands on Joey and stuffing his mouth with a sock, carrying him kicking to whatever jalopy he was driving now and heading off toward hell knows where. Dust would cover his tracks and I'd never see my boy again and I'd surely die. Because I'd think of him passed out with the winos in front of the Plasma Center, and people waking up from pass-out drunks on floors, and Violet lighting cigarettes off the stove burner, and Mexican TV, Davey'd shake his dwarf head and mouth off about the infernal heat under that big empty sky, and Buddy'd be asleep on the humpbacked recliner—his mouth open, flies crawling in and out. My son growing up like that, becoming one of *them.* It never once occurred to me that he actually loved the boy—it was simply not a consideration. Buddy expected a fight, surely, but he decided to risk it. Maybe he'd started believing his own lies—isn't that how it always goes with liars? He had it all figured, except for Dee.

Between us and the door, he waited for me to see him. Buddy Washer just stood there in his blue double-creased mailman trousers and scuffed shoes, that silly pith hat, kind of a smirk on his face, but something else—fear? or hope maybe, the two always got mixed up on his face. He could play from the cuff of either sleeve.

"Josephine."

"Buddy."

"How you been?"

"Good."

"The boy?"

"Joey."

"How is he?"

"Good."

"Sure is hot."

"Not really."

"You drawing more of them birds?"

"What do you want?"

"You back. Both of you."

"You're impersonating a postman."

He waved a letter, the way sombody'd wave a letter if inside it says they've got something real big on you. "Might be I really am the postman."

Joey'd come to me, was in my lap chewing a pencil, looking at his daddy with his daddy's eyes. He said, "Mama?" It was 4:30 or so in the afternoon, the street empty for heat. My sketch pad showed Joey's crooked bird smile, how one side of his mouth opened further than the other, a trait he'd share with Jimmy, his half-brother. Dee'd be home any minute, notebooks filled with numbers to add and subtract during pinto beans and cornbread. A way off past the river bridge, tall clouds were building for afternoon storms. They roll through and then it clears—steam rising off the green grass.

"How you think that makes me feel. Calling me a fake. I got a real letter here. For my flesh and blood son. It's signed by a judge."

Buddy held out his lie, waited for me to take it.

"My daddy'll kill you. He'll cut your head off."

Joey giggled, a little dab of spittle on his chin.

"I love you Josephine. In your heart, you know it's true. And you know I love my boy. How on earth can you not know?"

"Don't."

"Your heart knows."

When Joey was born, after my milk came, I lost a front tooth. A dentist said it happened sometimes. So here I was, twenty-one, about to be a single mom with my husband dressing up in his fake electrician clothes. Hanging out all day with who knows who—another woman and her baby, maybe—then threatening to drown me when I got wind of it. So I manage to scrape enough grit together and leave him and just about then, just as I was about to take Joey and put Arizona behind us forever, right on cue, an incisor falls out.

"Dee pay for that tooth? That's a lot better."

"Go to hell."

"Been there. I'm sorry."

"Leave."

"I got rights. Judge says so."

"I mean it. Leave now."

He cocked his hip and gave me that sideways look, just blocking our doorway, the shade playing on his neck and shoulders. Nobody on earth save us three. The air just went out of things and it was just us three in this vacuum. Only our puny voices. Me, with my too-white fake tooth, and Joey, who knew how bad this hurt him?—I've always heard the young bounce back. What next? More pathetic pictures of my son as a bird, crawling spirals and talking to the grass? Here was our ridiculous family tree of three. What a profound joke we must have looked like then at the beginning of August 1962. What an utterly crazy picture we must have made that day, Buddy with his hair combed back, tapping those mailman letters he'd faked on his palm, his mind running a mile-a-minute. He'd say whatever he had to say, do whatever had to be done—it was all that far along now, I could tell.

And me? Twenty-one, thinking my life was over—the me I used to be, sweet and trusting as white bread. All my life I've trusted people to a fault. For good or bad, that's how I'm wired. Maybe it's a Stepwell thing, that's the way it's always worked, and I know now—with full force—that it'll get me, it'll be my undoing sure as the world. So there we were in Arkansas: mother, father and child stuck in this crazy vacuum time-warp thing. I'd taken the little X-Acto knife out of my supply box and was fully prepared to cut Buddy's throat when Dee's car blared into the driveway. I held onto Joey and Buddy gave me that look, like his heart would break. And the hell of it is, I might have gone back to him. It's stupid, I know, but that's how I've always been, with O.W., and Shawn Terrence, the whole sorry lot. I don't know why.

There was lunging and screaming and Dee called the cops on the kitchen phone while we screamed at each other. Joey trembled and I held the artist X-Acto knife out in front of my face, the silver blade very bright and real. Across the street, a couple came out of their house. The man said, "Hey Mister, you need some help?"

Even when the police came, when they cuffed him and banged his head in the back seat of the squad car and his face seemed deformed behind the glass, when he screamed those things that I never wanted our boy to hear, I would've maybe gone with Buddy Washer even then. I later learned that it'd all happened during this killer tornado. The funnel was on the ground that instant—a swath of delta not seventy miles north. It plowed through Arkadelphia, howled down main street through the bank and post office where sixteen lay dead. As the cops drove my ex-husband out of my life forever, to the county pen and wherever he'd go after that, at that same time a tornado was smashing into this town's P.O., so that, as the story gets repeated, the mail got up into the jet stream somehow and, for years and years, people found stamped letters from towns like Searcy and Beebe and Dirty Devil, Arkansas fluttering down into Canada and the glittering icefields of the north.

5. Joey

We say our goodbyes in the driveway of the house on Third Avenue—the happy hour flag flying half-mast from yesterday. Cap hugs his daughter, weeps. We embrace awkwardly and stare down at the sprinkler-stained concrete. Bet and Rocky wave and blow kisses. Stern-faced Meg swats gnats. It's no longer possible to postpone: we back out onto the street, honk the horn and drive away.

This is how the party ends, Cap and Meg stand like stone pillars behind us.

Three blocks over at ocean side, Third Avenue beach access is a warped wood stairway, high as a lifeguard tower that commands a lookout over this fingernail of the Space Coast. White shoreline shines north to Cape Kennedy. A schooner in full sail glistens a few miles off like it's sailed out of some sea-going pastoral from a lost world, the sort Mama'd hang over the living room couch. This air is good to breathe. Down in the surf, the morning's surfers—sixteen-year-olds with immaculate tans and thin waists and gleaming hair—ride the last of the high-tide waves. One old-time fisherman, a straw-hatted geezer who carries photos of a twenty-pound Snook he landed here once, horses line out from a white surf rod. The night's turtle tracks are all but gone, though traces outline the base of a few dunes where I imagine eggs cracking open, the young about to crawl down against long odds. We sit wordless for a while, the salty air and birdsong—the summer-tanned youths riding out the green waves.

"Okay, sweetie. Honey, let's go."

Lara says, "*Stay.*"

She sits on the board rail between me and Renee. I breathe her hair in. I could weep now, long and hard. That's how I feel, like the moment we drive off a hard rain's going to fall, and the world will end—everything that's ever been for me, it's all about to be over. A parasail leaps colorfully over the horizon, the broad back of the world shining through. We're close now, my family. We've tanned. Renee's hair has lightened. She's taught Lara to swim these last few days, and that's good, very, very good. We cannot stay here any longer, not another minute, but the big water and all it encompasses—everything that's happened and not happened—holds us, holds me. For a little longer, we sit there and breathe between the road and the ocean.

The highway to Jacksonville goes past the Volusia County Sheriff's Detention Center, just outside New Smyrna Beach. Renee's on cruise control, debriefing herself from this family visit, the FM station playing one Tom Petty song after another. Lara's sacked out with her neck in a painful-looking angle in the car seat behind us. The Pathfinder's smooth, we're lucky to have it for the road, even if it is, now, officially stolen. We're technically in violation of state and federal law. Renee's talked herself deep into her family, up through how her brother Rocky worked off his jail time at this very place after the DWI when he was a student at FIT in Melbourne. The encampment stretches for miles along Highway 95— the poor bastards out there suffering the heat, hoeing the garden and sling-blading grass and shoveling shit outside Sheriff's horse barn.

The Rockersons, I learn, actually have a history of their men getting thrown in the poky. Uncle Elton went to Florida State on a swim scholarship, a full ride, only he got caught growing marijuana in the gutters of his dorm roof, which got him knocked out of butterflying and into Sheriff's ranch for six months. Nobody's supposed to talk about it, off limits entirely.

Her eyes sweep the ocean. "There's one story nobody's ever heard."

The story? What I'm thinking, deep in my gut, the question and the answer: what happens to a human body left half a day in 104 degree chlorinated hot tub water? What happened to my mama? Renee's voice rises. "You're supposed to say, 'What story?'"

I kill the radio. "What story?"

Cap was an Annapolis man, secretary for his 1954 Midshipman class. After War College and the move to California then Hawaii, he made Lieutenant then Lieutenant Commander before getting the nod for his first tour as full

Commander and CO on Destroyer Healey. The Navy's *up or out*, and Cap kept climbing. His second and third tours as Captain were commissioned out of Charleston. By then Renee was fifteen and Rocky was eleven. Life near a base was cake for boys, especially for officer's sons who could sneak keys to blasting zones and airplane hangars.

For Meg and Renee, stuck having to entertain dingbat officers' wives, it was a different deal altogether. For one thing, a military wife is judged primarily on her loyalty to her husband. You followed where you were led. Cap was at the top of his game—I've seen the photo's of him on deck in that startling white uniform and gloves, six-hundred sailors snapping to attention. This was 1970, we were at war, and the luck of a war is the sailor man's greatest gift, the messier the better. Cap sailed Destroyer Klaüs to the South China Sea, north from Ho Chi Minh City, where his ship was known to blow the shit out of Charley during one land assault after another. Word came down that a rank admiral had been passed over and Captain Rock C. Rockerson was to declare his desires.

"*Declare his desires,*" Renee says. "Can you believe that? It was toughest on Mom."

All the petty jealousies from the passed over officers' wives, all the afternoon teas that bled into evening cocktail parties, the martini glass flag flap-flapping in the sad light that washed in over Charleston Bay. The loneliness, always having to hold your tongue no matter how offensive and outright rude some people could be. There was one wife in particular who'd been pregnant that year and lost the child. She could be a real razorblade, that one, those things she'd say.

If Meg's travails were hard to bear, Renee's suffering was another flavor. She was in ninth grade that year, a drop-dead looker, and had made cheer squad at Goose Creek High. Sammy Davido was a junior halfback on the varsity team that lost two games up front, until he learned how to throw the half-back pass and the season got interesting. He was Filipino, a Catholic, and that never sat well with Cap. Anyway, all this was happening about the same time that the screenings began—the heat was on the whole family, it must have been something. Renee started sneaking out the bedroom window on Friday nights after the game, when the mown grass was just beginning to get that fall chill so that the dew was cold to her bare feet—that's what she remembers, cold feet and Sammy Davido's car in the dark beyond the circle drive. They'd cruise to the quarry and Sammy'd burn an incense cone on his dash, let his headlights shine out into the deep blue water where a girl had drowned the last summer, an enlisted man's daughter who drank Purple Jesus and split her head open diving off a cliff ledge. I've seen the photo Cap keeps in his office to this day of Renee then, that year, 1970. It's a profile shot; her hair shines down her back, straight and sleek, framing the flawless face that seems about to smile, but doesn't. Her shirt is long-sleeved white, worn outside her jeans. She's sitting and her arms are long and slender and capable of much work and love. The hazel eyes stare out, at the photographer I guess, and accuse or ask *why am I here*, or maybe just *fuck off*, which Renee's prone to be thinking—I've got a zillion pictures of her flipping off the camera. But Cap's photo, the one he keeps on his desk, it's stone cold.

Friday nights that October, the Goose Creek Gators would stomp the shit out of whatever cross-town rival and Sammy Davido'd rush for a hundred-and-eighty yards and score with the halfback pass. On the cinder track surrounded by Cheer Gators, she'd actually watch the game, see him looking at her from tailback position, through his face mask, the mouthpiece making his lips bulge. The carnival was in town, Homecoming week, and she was one of the Maids with a red corsage and two extra tampons in Sammy's letter jacket. That night held the thrill of overtime against the Oceanside Panthers. Goose Creek won by running Sammy up the middle—through the eight hole. Just before the big play, he'd stared straight at her—those dark eyes through her, it seemed—up on the glittery float with the White Goose Queen. Then he ran flat over the noseman for six points and got carried around on a lineman's shoulders. The war was about to end—there'd be no draft, the boys on the field wouldn't get killed by *gooks in the jungle*, Sammy'd said. She'd lept off the float and the cinder track was spongy beneath her feet—it made her knees go funny and the game was over. The R.O.T.C. cannon went off on the visitor's side and the band played the fight song loud into the fall night. Her and Sammy skipped out of the Homecoming dance that night after one slow number and drove to the quarry where the drowned girl's ghost had knocked on Shauna Fagg's fogged up window the week before—a ring of Purple Jesus around its mouth. She was on her period, so they couldn't do that, *no way José*, Sammy said. So it was the other, the thing she hated most, his hands still coated with the Stickum Coach had sprayed on to ward off fumbles, fraying the french braid her mother'd twisted for her tonight—the sweat and filth in the car's back seat and the forever feel of being pushed down and down and down. At the last minute, the tap on the window, Sammy's side, stopped what was happening. And even though she never saw it, the ghost girl's purple-stained lips—she's always believed that the enlisted man's daughter had somehow turned her life in a different direction.

One last thing—that fall, that October night after homecoming, after Sammy'd driven her back and not even kissed her good night, Cap was up, sitting at the kitchen table in the uniform he'd worn to work that morning. "Hey," he'd said. "How's my girl?"

"Tired."

"Good game tonight. How was the dance?"

"Just fine."

"Well, goodnight."

And Renee climbed the stairs and left him down there sitting, not doing anything, just sitting alone at the kitchen table with his hands in his lap. Later she'd learn what had happened that day, how Cap had been passed over—and the Navy was *up or out*, no two ways about it. A record of some weak inspection at sea had circulated, Cap was not to make admiral. A lot would happen before Christmas. She'd break up with Sammy Davido on a night when he stood outside under the nightlight, just stood there waiting her out. "Just go," she'd said after a while. He took a few steps, still wearing the half T-shirt from under his shoulder pads. He'd force her to remember this moment—in no uncertain terms—two weeks later, when she called after midnight to beg a ride to the jail downtown, where Cap was being held for DWI. Her mother, Meg, *was not to find out about this*, so Renee had to borrow bail money from Sammy as well. She had to see the look on Cap's face when she showed up with him at the jail, see Cap search the tile floor while Sammy and the deputy talked about last week's game, the problem in the passing attack. The war was all but over. She'd turn sixteen in

Maryland where Cap would get on with the Pentagon and they'd buy a nice tri-level outside the beltway and take summer trips to Chincoteague and Assateague where wild horses swim shallows between islands. Not long after we met, Renee took me out there, to Assateague National Seashore where we camped through a three-day thunderstorm and got plowed on vodka and cranberry juice. *Cape Codders for sailors' daughters*, she sang on a morning when the thunder drove us crazy and we could hear high tide breaking over the dunes.

Florida is one big, long blur, let me tell you. You can't see the ocean, but it's out there—all up 95 to Jacksonville Bay, where we hit an exit and fill up. Renee and Lara go potty while I do the windshield. When I check, the oil's bone dry—dead empty, we could have blown the head off our stolen Pathfinder. She takes all of four quarts, and I stash four more in the hatch just in case.

"Didn't you take care of that back at Pop's?"

"I thought so."

Lara says, "Why are we *here*?"

We take Highway 10 toward Live Oak and Tallahassee—the most dangerous road on the planet, the gas station man who sold me oil claimed. Driving east to west, the sun's bright in our faces. Afternoon comes on—my left arm burns through the window.

"Happy Father's Day, Daddy. You okay?" Renee reaches for my hand, squeezes it. Behind us, in the thrift shop car seat, our daughter's face is intense, she's coloring a gorilla purple, doing the giraffe upside down.

6. Josephine

Afternoons, we'd walk to MacArthur Park, not far from Dee's, where there was a swing and slide and big sweet black ladies pushing their babies in strollers with good luck mojos tied into their pigtails. This was summer, 1964, two years after the killer tornado when Buddy came dressed as the postman. Dee'd had him thrown in jail, but that hadn't stopped the last message, addressed to me, each letter thrumming. "Dead or alive?" it said, the strange handwriting slanted left, the letters falling west.

MacArthur Park had this grand museum built on the premises, a gift from the General's family. They kept a mummy inside behind a glass case, and Joey loved that, the mummy with writing that said he was a little boy, a prince who'd lived on the Nile in Egypt three thousand years ago.

"Is he happy in there?" Joey asked. "Is he hungry?"

The Pima County Library'd been thin on Egyptology, but I'd read how Pharaoh's priests packed food for the voyage to this imperishable place with a new heaven and earth, which was here I guess, *Arkansas*. How strange to have ended up here, the dead child riding a sun chariot across eternity to Pulaski County, Arkansas. But here he was, a little boy. Joey stared through the glass, playground sand in his shoes and the pretty black ladies laughed out loud at us and avoided the mummy at all costs, even though he was the museum's showcase piece—the big deal why tickets cost sixty-five cents. A light was fixed up above the little boy's head, or what looked like a head though it surely could not have been that anymore. Here were jars where organs and intestines were stored, a little dog whip and staff. We'd hold hands and just stand there looking, Joey asking other-worldy questions.

"What does he dream of?"

"I don't know, Joe."

"Can he leave if he wants?"

"I don't think so."

"Does mummy boy have a daddy? Where's his daddy?"

This was a Tuesday, the heat outside too much to take. Little black boys and pigtailed girls wandered in and out of the mummy room. "I don't know."

"What does his daddy look like?"

"He's tall," I said. "And he has strong arms for hugging."

"Is that postman my daddy?"

It's never what you expect that gets you. Never. When you get right down to it—*who am I? And who is my daddy? And just who are my people?* Isn't that what we're asking all our lives? Somebody tell me who I am, goddamnit, because something's not right here, I'm missing information. I'd been wrong not to tell Joey about Buddy and all the Arizona Washers. I'd have to come clean, to open up and let it all out, Buddy, Arizona, dwarf Davey and the see-saw trailer, eating dog—just come clean for my boy, shoot straight. And I knew that I wouldn't.

"Your daddy passed, Joey. He had an accident."

Joey tapped the mummy glass, let his chin fall. "I know Mama," he said.

"He was sweet and loved you with all his heart."

He shook his head, I could see his face in the glass. "No, he didn't."

My mascara was running. Children know the truth—their hearts don't lie. "He'd do anything for you."

"He hurt you."

"I love him."

Joey said, "I hate him."

And then he was gone. Disappeared. Right then and there with the old security guard clutching his hernia and goddamning the world to hell and my mascara running all down my blouse, Joey simply vanished. Out in the heat, past the swings and slides and sandboxes and big sharp-smelling sweetgum trees, women holding children tight to their chests, we searched for my baby, but he wasn't there. Inside again, frantic, my heart beating the way it does just before you die. In the mummy room the thought floored me—Joey'd somehow crawled into the mummy's wrappings, he was in there suffocating. Somebody called the police and they got me in the cop car, and I was crazy. I was shaking all over, the terror under the fillings in my teeth. I can taste it there this second. It came when Jimmy was killed, when the policeman knocked on the front door at two a.m., and I heard him out there shuffling his feet, and turned the porch light on and looked at him through the peephole, saw him playing with his wedding band, and the fear came down on me and crawled into my stomach where it's grown ever since.

Joey was gone, he'd disappeared into the other world he'd visited while I painted pictures in Dee's front yard, the water colors running off the page onto my thighs. And the policemen got me into the car and I could hear the radio chatter, and they asked me questions about who I was and who I knew and why was I here, and where on earth the daddy was. I knew that this was how it'd been for Buddy, his child taken, the cops on fire for answers. I don't know how, but my life caught up to me then, that Tuesday afternoon at MacArthur Park, just outside the little boy mummy's room. From the moment Buddy'd lied about the Arizona ghost girl and I'd bought the story, everything since then was my fault altogether. And the guilt would have killed me, would have just consumed me right then, had it not been for the beautiful brown-faced woman in the flower dress, standing in Dee's front yard with Joey in her arms. He was peaceful, already forgetting about the mummy and how I'd lied my head off that his daddy was dead. She gave him back, said "Lord, what a pretty boy, this one here." And that was that. Joey'd simply gotten out of the museum unseen, and walked the blocks back to Dee's. He'd crossed intersections, passed strangers and winos, had walked right up to this woman and reached out for her hand and she'd taken hold, just like he was a relative.

Why not? Why shouldn't there be sweetness in this world?

That very week I met O.W.

He was driving a Wonder Bread truck then, making a delivery at Tabor's Grocery on Thayer Street in a uniform. The name was written right there on the chest of his size nineteen long shirt. He smiled and nodded, stacking loaves on top shelves.

I smiled back, lingering between aisles. "Looks fresh."

"Better believe it."

He muscled another rack off his dolly, then stood up to his full height, six-two or so, the initials sewn in red right at my eye level.

"Ow," I said, like when you hurt. "I'm Josephine."

"It's O.W.," he said. "And this belongs to you." He held out a loaf of Wonder White Bread, a sandwich loaf that was soft and still a little warm and good smelling. His hands were big as split chickens. He could crush Buddy Washer's skull. And there was a sweetness about him.

I took the bread and said something dumb like, "Manna from heaven. But I can't just walk out with this. I'll have to pay."

"Nope," he said. "They know me here."

By week's end, he'd dropped off a bag full of cinnamon buns, bear claws, doughnut holes and twists. Joey was best man in our wedding, and later, after the adoption, we changed his last name to O.W.'s, Harvell. No one messed with us—we were left alone.

He'd have to meet Daddy, O.W. The duck club was ten-thousand acres of flooded timber between Wabbeseka and Humphrey. Stuttgart was Duck Capital of the World. Every fall they held this worldwide duck call contest and Miss Mallard got driven down Main Street on the hood of a Corvette, her green sash fluttering in the breeze amongst the sky calls and sixteen gauge shotguns going off out over flooded rice fields. The bright sky would sometimes darken with ducks, their silver wings whistling. Unlike Jefferson and Monroe Counties, Arkansas County was wet— hard liquor was to be had. Men who expected to stand five hours in chest-deep ice water needed whiskey—I can understand that entirely. They call it still-hunting. Still hunts are like little deaths—see how long you can stay still, pretend not to be.

My daddy and his second wife, Ruby, had driven down from Morrilton after Christmas dinner to set camp before New Year's. That was opening day, when the big money rolled up from New Orleans—these red-faced men in rental cars filled with ribeye steaks and George Dickel, they'd roll in half happy, ready to shoot something. The building was a cinder block job with four cold bedrooms full of bunkbeds with those tree-shaped air-fresheners hung up under the box springs. Ruby'd stack towels at the foot of each bed, along with a box of Remington number four magnums, a bag of peanuts and pint bottle of Ancient Age—gifts from the host, Daddy, who'd get tipped two-hundred dollars a man when it was all said and done. A huge fireplace lit up a half-dozen mounted mallards and wood ducks, along with a six-pound crappie and somebody's Boone & Crockett citation whitetail deer, green Christmas tinsel strung between tines. Above the kitchen stove hung a collection of cast iron cookware such as might never be seen outside the fish shacks and duck clubs of the Arkansas delta.

Out back, a room was heated for waders, a dozen pairs of them hanging like little upside down men. I used to go out there when I was a girl, after Daddy had his leg cut off and got hooked on morphine. After the divorce. See the afternoon sun in winter come through a window that looked out over a turnip field to the west, beyond which stretched Bayou Meto, where Daddy'd float his flat bottom on days before season, between Christmas and the New Year. We'd string yo-yos baited with live shiners set four feet deep for crappie. Daddy'd scull the flatbottom through the stumpy water, from one tripped yo-yo to the next, unhook crappie and smallmouth and the stray blue channel, throwing them flop at my feet. Once, on a morning when the sky glowed pink and orange, the air went simply black with mallards, a whole world of them. A whole world of ducks. The sound of their wings beating air, their voices grainy and hilarious so we got fall-down laughing sick, both of us, me and Daddy, him a little happy, maybe, a snort in his morning coffee. This is where I took O.W. after he married me. Joey, me, and my new husband O.W.—four days between Christmas and New Year's, 1965.

Ruby'd got a lard ass. In the four a.m. pitch black, her side of the flatbottom dipped low, so O.W. had to sit as far as he could on the opposite side up front to balance. Daddy knew the invisible bayou channels. When low branches slapped O.W. in the face he'd say, "goddamnit," in that low-mean voice. And sometimes Daddy'd laugh out loud. Me and Joey snuggled between them, these men with shotguns on their laps. It was dark, an ungodly hour before day and cold enough for skim ice on the channel. Daddy cut through three miles of flooded timber, out to the clear pools where trees thinned enough for mallards to see the decoys when the sun came up. My father was outright famous across three states, I knew, for how he piloted the flatbottom through dark sloughs, wide open turns into the darkness he knew by heart. Everybody tipped the Jesus out of him for that, knowing the dark by heart. And he did it full-throttle with a forty-horse Mercury. Christ knows how fast we went, branches slapping O.W. silly up front, those gut-low curses that kept Daddy in stitches. I hung tight to Joey and scooted us both close to Ruby whose butt wasn't going anywhere. No moon and no stars that morning, just dark and cold in our faces, the high-pitched motor every now and then hitting a root, threatening to shear pins.

Daddy cut the motor and let the boat glide into a spot about the size of an ice rink. Steam was rising in the quiet—like the insides of something, mummy boy, maybe. Quiet as the deepest, darkest place. Joey'd just turned five—the magic year, I'd learn. We all sat there breathing while it got light enough to make out mallard decoys, special magnets inside of them so they'd pair up. My father loaded his Browning, told O.W. to do the same. Metallic *shrings* rang out when the guns' chambers jammed shut—final and real. O.W. slid off the bow, breaking ice.

"Shit," he said, black water to his chest.

Daddy got in, drew the call from the string around his neck and sounded. Bursts squawked up through the tree tops. One man started wading and the other followed. O.W.'s shotgun lay over his right shoulder, he'd never duckhunted a day in his life. They caught a slough rut that ran out catty-corner to the east where light was coming now.

"Tell me what happened, sugar." Ruby said. "With that Buddy."

Daddy'd given Joey a Yentzen caller, and he was fooling around up in the bow, moving, trying not to freeze. Ruby'd brought coffee in a thermos, but we had only the cap for a cup, and so took turns sipping and pouring. The sun was rising.

"He tried to kill me." The words came out a whisper.

"*No.*"

"Yeah."

Ruby tilted her head. She was sweet and had been pretty once, I could tell. Joey's eyes were off in the clouds, maybe he wasn't listening, maybe he couldn't hear. "How come?"

Three gunshots—loud, then a muffled echo. "What are they doing?"

Two ducks winged up the corridor—their wings going *tu-tu-tu*. A fox squirrel barked up an oak. Something splashed, then a woodpecker, the huge

Pileated kind, went off. Joey hung off the front of the boat, making faces in the water—in his zone, his place. Gunshots followed gunshots. And then some wild thing would appear like a bat out of hell, gone as quick as it came.

"In a quarry."

"They have those in Tucson?"

"A spring," I was whispering, looking at Joey, my son, how he looked like Buddy and me mixed. "Under these red cliffs."

"I'll be."

Joey held the boat paddle in the slack water, sculling, watching us out of the corner of his eye. The woodpecker hammered a cypress. O.W.'d agreed to adopt Joey, to give my boy his name. What would he say to Daddy?

"He'd lied about a job. Every morning he got up and dressed like he was a ground electrician. Then he went somewhere and stayed all day. I don't know where. His brother Davey the dwarf, he told me Buddy had a second wife. And they had a baby. He knew I was leaving, taking Joey."

"Your daddy doesn't know that. How'd you get out?"

Off in the distance I could hear the men sloshing, my husband and my father, my son catching light in the bow, saying words now into water, his lips forming little syllables and vowels.

"He kept saying he loved me." Joey's eyes were on mine—his own voice barely making sounds. "Davey was with us. We all just climbed out and didn't say anything. He knew I was taking Joey away from there. He took me out there to kill me. But he backed down. He kept talking about love."

"Did you love him still?"

"Yep."

"How?"

Daddy was in front, three green heads strung off his belt, wingtips just skiffing the water. O.W. behind, a pair of green heads, walking the way a man walks after he's killed. "*He'll do*," Daddy said. "You look chilly-willy, Joey. Looky here." Daddy handed Joey his gun, said be careful. Then he climbed in and we almost all went under. When O.W. was on board, we all sat quiet for a minute, the sun filtering through the trees. A flock of geese passed overhead in a big V, their feathers all lit up and shining like angel's wings.

Daddy said, "Knock'em out, John," and fired up the Mercury. A low branch slapped O.W. when we turned into the channel.

"Goddamn it."

"Sorry Charley," Daddy said, that Stepwell grin.

And that was that. If the men didn't exactly hit if off, they tolerated each other. O.W., Daddy no doubt knew, was not somebody to mess with. He'd make Joey a father and Buddy'd never dare come around, I believe my daddy knew this. Daddy'd never bought Buddy Washer's load of crap, he'd seen through him up front and I'd married against his wishes. *He'll do*, what my daddy said.

That night we ate a king's feast, roast mallard with gravy and dirty rice, turnips steeped in butter and bread crumb, purple hull peas Ruby'd canned herself. I was pregnant with Jimmy, gorging for two. The men got snockered on bourbon and played poker on the big wooden table. The fire burned all night while they told their hunt stories and their waders hung upside down, leaking little puddles in the dark out room. 1966 rolled in, us all dancing outside under a haloed moon that predicted snow.

And it did snow—six inches on New Year's Day.

Stepwell tradition necessitates going outside barefoot on mornings like this, don't ask me why. All my life, it's been Daddy and Uncle Waylow dancing around whatever clapboard renthouse we shared. MaMa Stepwell, my grandmother even, the snow curling her hair. And that's what we all did that morning not far from Stuttgart, Arkansas. Dizzy and cold before the bowl games started, we danced ourselves around the cinder block duck club—honest joy pounding in my heart. I've never been sure what O.W. made of my daddy—he plays the cards close to the chest. Maybe he felt like he had to compete with Daddy—men are like that, jealous of anything with a dick.

Daddy took the lead, hopping under the big grey sky on one enormous bare foot. I followed, Joey in tow. O.W. shook his head when we followed Daddy for a second lap. "You're all crazy," he said.

"*Good* crazy," Daddy told him. "We're *good* crazy."

7. Joey

Sometimes Renee suffers from laughing sickness. We'll be in a restaurant, anywhere you're supposed to be quiet, and something will happen. Maybe we've just ordered fettuccine down at Gepetto's, a place with lackluster food and music for happy hour in the big front room that overlooks 13th East and the foothills out over the Wasatch Range. So we've ordered and the salads are about to come, and we know the lettuce will be iceberg so we're not enthused. We *cheers* and sip five-dollar glasses of jug wine. And something's about to happen, both of us know that, we learned long ago to read one another's minds. I feel her waiting and she me, it happens all the time. Anyway, Gepetto's has live music. A woman sits up by the fireplace mantel on a stool with a guitar in her lap. She's looking straight at us, moving her lips, smiling. Renee's got her back to this woman, so I nod hello—*yes, I see you*. Renee looks over her shoulder—the three of us connect. We're the only people in Gepetto's, the food's not good and no one else is here. Our iceberg salads arrive, blue cheese over the croutons. This lady up by the wall is smiling, moving her lips. I nod again, Renee turns again, we all three see each other again.

This is when it starts.

"Good *evening*," the lady up by the fireplace says. "Do you know who I am?"

Renee snorts. This is all it takes—crazies approach us all the time, if there's an insane person in the house, they'll float our way, me and Renee, we're magnets for the mentally ill.

Now, we avoid each other's eyes. That's the key, don't look at Renee when laughing sickness is about to start.

"*You-hoo*," the lady sings. She strums a G-chord at us. "I asked you, do you know who I am? Do you know what I'm famous for?"

The *famous* part gets to Renee. She looks me in the eyes, only for a second. She's trying to chew iceberg lettuce with her mouth shut, tears just starting at the corner of either eye. Her face flushes—this is not about me.

The famous lady strums the G and hums. She says, "You don't have to talk to me unless you want to."

Renee swallows, takes a sip of jug wine that immediately comes out her nose. She's history. We both are.

"*Doo-doo-doo*," the lady goes. "I wrote that song, the Kodak film song. You know, 'The Times of Your Life.' It's bigger than the Beatles."

Like I said, just us three in the room. The light's good outside, it's happy hour and this woman who wrote the Kodak film song is entertaining us at Gepetto's. We don't have to talk unless we want. Renee is giving it all she's got, fighting tears, her breaths coming out in little gusts. Then it happens. Iceberg lettuce spills with the first note, a high laugh rising up and infecting me. Once it starts, there's no point in holding back. This is the time of your life, these three minutes with the Kodak film lady. By the time our mealy fettuccine arrives, we're wasted. Another couple comes and the whole thing starts again. Lord help us, we're saved: *know who I am?*

A certain kind of laughter is the acknowledgment of death, I've read. And some people laugh at inappropriate moments. I don't know why this comes to me now in the Pathfindner, Renee and laughing sickness, "The Times of Your Life" woman going *doo-doo-doo*. Today's Father's Day; rocketing toward me my whole life, this long drive home.

By the time we hit Pensacola Beach, Lara makes it clear that this is the end of the line, as far as we go. I've been here once before, with an old girlfriend who was an emergency room nurse and traveled with a long roll of little blue Valium that made you pass out in the sun with all the other rednecks and fry yourself to Jesus. We arrive on the heels of a rain, you can see the squall line receding east, the way we've just come. Our hotel for the night is to be a place called Sandy Shoes, one of those blue-painted clapboard beachsides. A sliding glass window and two plastic chairs on a cracked patio. This could be the same place as that other time with a girlfriend, when we got whacked on Valium and Coors

Lite and I broke out the glass door—just walked right into it, *whammo*. While she went out for stone crabs and shrimp, I called home collect. Mama was in St. Vincent's with kidney stones. She was to have the "basket procedure" the next day, sleepy Traceleen said on the other end. I remember because it was August 25th, Jimmy's nineteenth and final birthday, and it seemed odd for her to be having a stone then. I had to get home. We hit the highway arguing after crabs and more beer. The girlfriend paid with American Express and we drove on out listening to Bad Company. We said things, and the worse it got, the faster she drove. Like a bat out of hell, she blew past semis in a thunderstorm, these big waves of rainwater walloping the windshield. By Mobile I'd had it, "Just let me out," I said, and that's just what she did, just pulled right over to the curb. She drove away and she never came back. I remember standing there, not believing it had happened. Then I traded my wristwatch to a cabdriver for a ride to the bus station, where people like me always ended up, standing at the payphone saying, "I'll pay you back. You know me. Please, just this one time."

But this night is easy. We order a pizza and eat on the patio looking out at the gulf where a couple dolphin surface minute to minute. Sunday night, we've hit on slow time, the place is dead save a few construction workers drinking beer three units down. I've backed the Pathfinder in up front so the plates don't show. Tomorrow's a new day. I'm going home. This is when the salt taste starts, right there in Pensacola on the day we've driven up and across Florida, followed the Spanish trail through the heart of the state. I'm staring out at the still gulf, drinking vodka and tonic with Renee, Lara chewing limes.

"This pizza's too salty."

Inside our lawn chair circle, the pizza box yawns open and closes in the after storm-breeze. Lara's fixated on the dolphins that cruise the shallows out in the low tide. It occurs to me that we're just right for sunset. We face West, where our real home is two thousand miles away in mountains where frost falls on sage.

"Not really," Renee says. "Maybe it's just salty in your head still."

"Does it make a difference. Inside your head or out?"

"Hard question. Lara, don't eat those limes."

"I've been here before."

Renee says, "I've been feeling that way all day. Ever since we left the beach."

"A long time ago."

The construction workers are laughing. Lara points and smiles, gets this look on her face that reminds me of me. "Dad," she says, "looky." Beyond the construction workers, across the uneven lot, a stork waddles. "He's so funny."

Tonight Mama will speak to me the way the dead speak in the dreams of grieving people. I don't know this yet, how time will get all holy. How the dead rise up, appear themselves entirely and say, "It's okay, sweetie," and offer pertinent sympathy and understanding for the griever. Sometimes they tell jokes, about salt in your mouth, maybe. Mama'd be like that, a joke-teller, *hey, the time of your life—know who I am?* Then comes the punch line. Isn't that the whole theory of laughter anyway? Wasn't that a *New Yorker* essay, before I canceled? Laughter, our best *mojo*, running interference between life and death? Already in my head, starting to form there though I don't know it, the drop dead fact that I'm going to get up on a stage in front of Mama's casket and deliver her eulogy. I'll have to face O.W. I'll look him in the eye and see what's there. Trace will be there, I'll see the whole Lonoke County lot, maybe even peckerhead Shawn Terrence Lord who'll sit way in back, scared shitless—with good reason—of O.W. Uncle Bold and Aunt Judy'll be there, and O.W.'s little brother, who weighs three hundred pounds and once pitched for the St. Louis Cardinals. All the Stepwells will look up at me from the pews. The Arizona Washers, who knew, maybe Buddy'd show up with a foil-wrapped dog. The preacher, Brother Dellwood, he'll be behind my back, very Baptist, which is the worst of the worst of the worst, believe you me. And he'll want to turn Mama's death—her corpse—into an opportunity for sinners to get salvation, some way to make them choke on guilt and hurt real bad. He'll ask us to imagine burning in hell for all eternity. The bastards—they'll do it every single time. When Jimmy died, him laying in that open casket with his eyes and lips sewn shut with that fine- clear thread, Brother Dell'd looked me straight in the face the whole time he delivered the Cain and Abel sermon. It was something, really, how his eyes glowed when he threw his head back and shouted, "Oh Cain where is thy *brudder*?" And me about half in shock like everybody else, beside Mama, the way her chin quivered. The embalmers who'd stolen his Rolex watch, they'd had to reconstruct part of Jimmy's face. The whole thing—it was just too fucking much. And Brother Dell Cain and Abling me, then offering the call to salvation, looking me straight in the eye—*this is your fault and you know it, don't you, you sad little fuck?* And, you know, I believed him for a while. In the hollow of my bones I felt it was so.

A couple friends had driven down to the funeral from Fayetteville, Ray Ray and Dirky Lee high on whiskey and road food. Ray Ray hadn't brought shoes, so I gave him a pair of Jimmy's. Together, they sat up in the balcony looking down on the silver casket and me—beside Mama on the first pew—riveted to Brother Dell while he Cain and Abled me. Dirky Lee was so moved that he wrote the whole scene down, *verbatim*, for a novel, all the way to Jimmy crashing his car into a tree stump, a fact Dirky jazzed up by making him naked in a Trans Am. It's his ending scene, his *finalé*, for Jesus sake.

"Cain? Where is thy brudder?"

Brother Dellwood, I'll have to contend with him, and I'm not entirely ashamed to tell that contending with Brother Dellwood Walker was an event I could almost look forward to. *Salvation*, my ass. How about slay him with laughter? "How about them apples?" what Mama always said. Get down to the root of all things—*laughter and slaughter.*

It's dark when I wake up, and I about half expect for the phone to ring and somebody else I love to be dead. My daughter's tonsils are enlarged; her breathing is raspy, like how Uncle Waylow used to sound in the camper down in the Fordyce deer woods. Beside me, Renee smells like home, she's my Mama now.

All my life—I've said it—I've loved angry women.

O.W.'s blood-type was O-negative, rare in our state, so he was all the time getting phone calls in the middle of the night for carwreck victims and amputees—victims of sudden violence who were that second teetering at death's door. I've since read that O-negative is a trait leftover from Cro-Magnon man, heavy-muscled hunters whose brains evolved for the kill. Whatever, O.W. wasn't selfish about his blood— one heavy bleeder named Polly something sent post cards thanking us every Christmas. One was in his front pocket on the night he retrieved me from Pleasure

Bowling Lanes Kiddo Alley with his head split open. He just walked right in and hauled me out, smelling of beer and Pall Mall, blood greasing the back of his skull down onto a bowling shirt with O.W. stitched into its chest.

Outside in the parking lot, somebody threw a beer bottle, then squealed off.

"Your day will dawn," O.W. said, not a trace of anything in his face. There'd been some kind of fight, I'd learn, and a man had pulled a tire iron.

Mama was in the car, a junker O.W.'d bought for their wedding. He got some rubber on Asher Drive, then hauled ass up to the railroad crossing at Vine and Thayer. There, O.W. killed it, pulled his key, got out and shut the door. "How about them apples," I heard him say.

The headlights were on—they sprayed him straight in the back, gore soaking half his shirt now. He looked back and hard light shone in his eyes–it was how fire must have once looked in a cave man's eyes. And there we were, me and Mama on a railroad track.

I said, "Mama?" She was humming this song from an album called *The Moon Over Naples*. The album cover had a gondola boat floating on water shimmering under the moonlight. It was a sweet melody, a little sad, just right for Mama's humming voice. She scooted over to the driver's seat, the notes trilling in her throat. When she turned off the headlights O.W. disappeared. Then her keys jingled and the engine started. Mama drove us off the railroad track, hung a U-ie and headed home. We walked into our dark house and she tucked me into bed with a stuffed dog that still smelled like vomit from Spring flu.

She said, "Don't ever be like him."

The phone was ringing off the wall. I said, "I like that song."

"Thanks, Joe," she said. "Sleep tight."

Then I shut my eyes for a while, listening to her shower, the sounds of water falling and the rise and fall of her voice humming the moon song. She was pregnant, and I picture her taking care not to slip when she got out of the shower. I see her drying herself with a pink towel, one foot raised to the tub, nice steam clouding the mirror. At first, the noise of the carport door being kicked off its hinges might have belonged to somebody else's house. Then, for what seemed like a long time, it sounded like this monster was ripping the skin off the front of our house.

In my room, Mama breathed hard in my face. She said, "It'll be okay." In the dark, I heard the little click, my door locking. Then she locked herself into their bedroom where I imagined her reaching for something heavy to swing, something with honest heft. Pieces of the front door skittered up the hallway. There was this quiet moment, long enough to wonder if it had gone away.

Then Mama's door burst. The sound was awful. Something crashed into the sheetrock wall and I heard him hit her. "*Get help, Joey,*" Mama screamed. "*He's killing me.*"

Paralyzed, I lay in bed. I was six years old, scared little shitass. Years would pass before I'd dream myself breaking his neck, see the shiver in his eyes when the cord severed. I lay there and listened to the hitting and choking and cussing. Next day, she'd walk around with cover stick over her eyes, saying she'd run into a wall or something. And he'd be laid open cheek to chin by a fingernail.

I wonder what it must have taken for her to ask that, to plant those words in my head: *Get help. He's killing me.*

Beside me, Renee smells like home. The sun will shine today and we'll make our way out of this in-between place. *Fuck Dirky Lee*, what does he know anyway. Some day I'll thank him right. *Fuck everybody*, that's what O.W.'d said. I'm on my feet before I know it, punching the cinder block wall in the room with my sleeping wife and daughter. *One, two three*—the thwacks sear up my forearms.

Out of the corner of my eye, Renee lifts her head. I see her see me— something passes between us. "What on earth, Joey? Are you crazy?"

Lara's been fitted for hearing aids, though we've held off. She sleeps mouth agape, the air rasping in and out.

"Dirky, Dell, O.W.," I say. "*Fuck everybody.*"

8. Josephine

Joey's best friend then was this Catholic girl named Melody whose mother taught piano up Shelley Street. She carried a Ouija Board with her at all times, and was always predicting the end of the world, either by fire or famine or heretofore unknown pestilence. Joey and Melody scooped stringy flesh out through the hole I'd cut in the thing's head, despite my boss's warning that Halloween was heyday for neurologists sewing up severed wrists. I separated out seeds for baking. A good idea, Melody claimed, since the whole world was about to go kabang and eating pumpkin seeds was known to get you reborn into the next.

"Who tells you this?" O.W.'s old transistor radio was staticky, but I could still make out Marty Robbins singing "My Woman, My Woman, My Wife" like he really meant it.

"Otto."

"Otto?"

"Otto." The olive-skinned girl pointed a finger at the glossy board by her feet, the one glass eye just now lighting up the cursive letter D. She said, "He knows."

"Tell me all about it."

"The end is nigh."

"Nigh?"

"Nigh."

I'd never cooked pumpkin seeds, nor considered the possibility of using the word *nigh* or consulting spirits on game room boards. Joey'd camped out in the back yard a few times with Melody. Had they practiced witchcraft? Satan worship? Sex? Some Catholic version of the three combined? "So Melody, how's it going to happen."

She looked at me through pale blue eyes, little yellow flecks all lit up. "Like a thief in the night," she said. "You'll never know what hit you."

Somebody down the street was burning pine needles, a bitter-sweet smell. Not yet dark, the stray ghost already wandered Shelley Street, holding its daddy's hand in one hand and a plastic pumpkin bucket in the other. My first batch of oil-soaked seeds was already in the oven—an experiment on getting us into the next world—at 350 degrees. I was pregnant. Hadn't O.W. tried to make up for parking us on a railroad track and kicking doors down? He paid cash for a repo-convertible with good smelling seats and shiny bumpers, so nobody could look down their noses at me when I parked outside of Our Lady's, waiting for my son to walk out through the big oak double doors. We had a house, with a pine thicket growing between us and Highway 40, which rolled west towards Texas and New Mexico and Buddy Washer.

"*Boo.*" His voice came from around the corner.

Joey said, "*Daddy.*"

And there was O.W., wearing one of those little silly Zorro masks, bizarre with his flattop. He laid this enormous bread bag at the foot of the table where some of the pumpkin goop had dripped. Out spilled a half-dozen of the most heavenly honeybuns.

"How's Spider Man?" he said and hauled Joey up in his arms.

It was just the right moment, the perfect time, really, with October and burnt pine needles in the air, the vampires and witches wayward between houses. In a few minutes the house would fill with smoke from scorched seeds—yet another danger to be added to Dr. Conn's wacky pumpkin theories. But for then, in the gold light with O.W.'s honeybuns tumbling onto the patio outside the sliding glass doors, a sliver of new moon had just risen, Marty Robbins sang "My Woman, My Woman, My Wife," with his whole heart. Melody scooped up two buns. "Thank you Mr. Harvell," she said and started running. Away from us and up the street. Melody ran, a honeybun shining in either hand.

"Daddy?" Joey said, the light in his face like his father's. He pointed at the ground. "What about Otto?"

"Otto who?" O.W. said, an edge creeping into his voice.

At our feet, the glass eye had slid onto bare concrete, and I tried reading nothing into that, but then the smoke hit us and it was time to clean up and for Joey to become Spiderman. I keep picturing O.W. out in the backyard in the Zorro mask, banging burnt pumpkin seeds off the baking sheet. All the doors flung open, our house full of smoke. The last gold light catching his face, that silly black mask crooked over his eyes.

We lived for a while out Arch Street Pike, in an old rickety two-story with big white columns in front and a back pasture for haying. There was a barn with piles of white pea gravel that O.W. hauled up to Lanty and spread over the Stepwell graves. Me and O.W., Joey and Jimmy lived in the big rent house with walnuts and yellow roses and, growing way back in the back pasture, a muscadine vine grew up the side of an oak, twenty or thirty feet into the sky. The wild grapes ripened before fall, so that sparrows would light high up in the vines late of the afternoon. They'd suck juice from sun-fermented berries and get snockered as Cooter Brown. Those afternoons, me, Joey and Jimmy would sit out in the back pasture bitter weeds and watch sparrows suck muscadine wine until—one at a time—they'd fall from the high spot clear to the ground. These little birds falling, they'd thud on the ground and lay knocked out for a while, then stand up, shake dust from their silver wings and fly up again. The funniest thing.

So we lived in this gargantuan rent house nobody'd insure. A hundred years old, the place was wood frame with pine floors that shone if scrubbed. The fuse box hissed and popped and all the big white columns out front had wood rot. But the countryside was out of this world—we had room to breathe and the boys could grow up outside in the pastures where wild grapes grew up the sides of trees and even the birds seemed drunk on love. We could have horses, chickens, maybe hay the back pasture. Everything seemed game. O.W. got on with Greyhound Bus Lines and we got free tickets for an actual vacation to sunny California. Some of Dee's people had moved west in the great migration of Arkies and Okies during dustbowl times, so we had relatives out there with orange trees and avacados growing in their yards.

O.W. was a dashing Greyhound man, dressed in blue trousers and ironed shirt, the hat all jaunty like an airline captain. He'd say into the driver's microphone, "Next stop, Hot Springs. Famous for hot water and horses." His speaking voice would be sweet and deep. "Please visit McClard's Barbecue," he'd say. "Where you'll save ten-percent with your charter stub." Five days a week he ran to Oaklawn Downs, this big tour bus full of amateur gamblers in bright sweaters, people from the Heights and Cammack Village with money to burn. O.W.'s a good driver—he'd keep it steady while they sipped champagne and scribbled on scratch sheets, divining longshots, tri-fectas and daily-double combos. He can be gentle that way when he likes. To be sure, my husband—O.W.—was the most luckless gambler I've met. He couldn't pick a horse if it walked up and bit him on the butt, but he was persistent, give him that, he kept trying. He'd lose a week's paycheck in a day, then pawn his .30 ought-six. Then he'd lose the next week's pay and kite a check for in-between money. Of course, when I got wind of what he was doing, when we damn near got evicted from our run-down mansion, I raised Cain. We had a real fight then, all that open interior space for a battlefield; we've both got tempers. I could've killed him, but then the Greyhound tickets came through. O.W. brought them home in a white envelope with a loose yellow rose. "I'll stay here and work to catch us up," he said, a fingernail cut oozing a little down his jawline. "You three have fun."

Two twenties and a ten were tucked inside. "Where'd this come from?"

"I love you," he said. O.W. touched my eye. "It won't happen again."

All my life, I've believed.

Dee's niece, Juanita, had been burned terribly as a young girl in a house fire, but she'd grown up fine and become a city planner in L.A., which seemed helter-skelter as any place could ever be. She was a riot, Juanita, picking us up at the downtown station, the traffic out of this world, driving with nubs at the ends of her arms, chainsmoking, punching the radio buttons from Merle Haggard to Miles Davis to the weather. "When's this fucking high pressure gonna break," she said with this big horsey laugh and real smile. "How about Chinese?"

Jimmy'd started to stutter by then, his chin locking into that hard cramp, the words all choked up inside. And Joey? Who knows about him—he's always lived in his own world, though sometimes I got close enough to get a glimpse. He'd passed fifth grade, but started these stunts that alarmed his teachers. Once he took a deck of cards into class, handed it Miss Blue, and told her to pick one. For some reason, she did, while he was out at recess, and locked it in her top drawer. "He said King of Hearts," she whispered into the phone. "How'd he know that?" like he was king of the underground or some such. Stuff like that. But Joey was my man, even then—try talking to somebody about your firstborn, try to explain.

Juanita was Dee's sister's son's daughter, which made her who knows what to me, Joey and Jimmy, but she was good people, honest to the bone. The happiest person I've ever known—bar none, not one bit disfigured inside, Juanita was my soul mate, my heart's kith and kin.

"Leave the son of a bitch," she said over a mound of fried rice in her apartment, not far from the ocean. "Wake up some morning and pour rat poison in his oatmeal. Put a gun to his head. They have laws about this—his ass's in a sling. Don't you know? Want a pistol, cuz?"

"O.W. takes care of me," I heard myself say, amazed deep down that we'd made it this far, to California, where my boys were just now munching egg rolls and Admiral's Chicken. This was before Traceleen, my daughter; I still felt young then, but I feel young now—chew on that one.

"Why'd you come here?" Juanita clicked chopsticks with what was left of a hand.

"To get away."

"From what?"

"Can we see the ocean? Can I swim in the ocean?"

"Oh you." Juanita said, "Sure, cuz."

After dinner she piled us all back into her car, as she would for the rest of the week until O.W. called and said that something was up—it was time to come home. I remember watching her, how the scars were papery over her cheek and down her neck, blooming over her arms and fingerless hands. She smiled, seeing me see her, touched my elbow and nodded. "See there," she said.

In front of us, wide open ocean, the end of the road. Out where the surf broke, both boys grinned, body surfed. "Ma-ma-ma." Jimmy pointed at a man in a crewcut, flying a kite with a jet silver tail. "Da-Da-Da-Daddy," he said.

Before we left, Juanita handed me this little baggy of yellow powder. "Use this when you need to. Give him the whole goddamn business," she said. I dumped it out in a bus station toilet, just outside Tucson where saguaro cactuses still looked for the world like men whose arms twisted into the sky. When I dialed information, a voice said it was unlisted at the owner's request. "Here's where I had you, Joey," I said.

It was almost sunset, the sky breaking tangerine orange out over the Sonoran Desert. A thin dirt devil shimmied over the mesa, behind it Mt. Lemon, the snow cap that had bewildered me so many years before. "Out there? My daddy's out there?"

9. Josephine

You get to know people on the bus. The driver let Joey and a boy whose name won't come sing on the microphone up front, this kid mocked Jimmy's stutter, kept saying d-d-daddy. I shared a seat with a woman who'd ridden west with us on this same bus, a week earlier. We shared histories, the small and humongous things that disgusted us about men, baby pictures, what we'd be if we could be anything on earth.

"Rich," I said.

"In love," she said. "Mary Kay driving a pink Cadillac."

"Double trouble," I said.

"Mother Teresa."

"The happy hooker."

Jimmy was an honest genius, real smart, but people cocked their heads when he talked, all those hard consonants locking down. Over the microphone up front, the queer little singer boy mocked Jimmy's stutter, kept saying *d-d-d-daddy*. And it dawned on me we were going back again, O.W.'d called saying it was time to come home. *I can't tell you why*, he'd said. Isn't life just one goddamn hilarious roaring good time. I'm good natured. I have a sense of humor, even with all the bullcrap. And that's very necessary for living. Have a sense of humor. Stay on the sunnyside. By Fort Smith we had the same driver who'd driven us part way out. I was sitting beside this new, old friend— maybe telling her about the day my daddy got his leg cut off, or how to make chocolate gravy and biscuits.

"It's hell, ladies, idn't it," the driver said out of the blue, his bright pink mouth stretched over the yard-long rearview.

"What do you mean? How so?" we asked.

"Week ago, week and a half, I drive you out of Little Rock, and very next thing your house burns to the ground. A hell of a thing."

"Lord." I said, "God." I thought he meant the woman next to me—her house, and started blurting how we'd help out, get some money together and clothes and toothbrushes. Tomatoes, I said, I don't know why. This sticks to my ribs, how I reached out and touched the woman's face, how it was new after all these miles. One of those ripcords in time that sticks, you know you've been moving toward it all along, and then it's there, right in front of your face.

In the big square rearview, the driver's face went white.

"Honey," this lady, my new friend, said. "It ain't me."

The driver kept his mouth shut after that, so me and the boys were driven from Alma down through Clarksville and Morrilton where the Stepwell family cemetery overlooks a pasture with a lightning-struck tree. We had hours to wonder, imagine skin burning, as if Juanita back in California had somehow got into the future and burned O.W. with her fire.

But there he was, O.W., at the terminal. He held onto me for a long time under a sign that advertised *Good Times, Tulsa.* And the next day and the next we sifted ashes with window screens borrowed from neighbors two pastures down. He'd escaped wearing only his underwear, one coal falling from the ceiling onto his chest, just above his heart, searing the hole that woke him and saved him before the ceiling collapsed. He had walked out of the burning house in his skivvies, started my ragged convertible and pulled onto Arch Street Pike, not knowing where to go or what to do. A grown man in underwear, driving through stoplights with a hole burned into his chest. His family off in California with a burned up woman who parlayed poison his way. That was O.W.—for him, fire's no friend.

We sifted our ashes and moved on. To Lonoke this time, a small town some thirty miles north and east of Little Rock. We got Jesus there at the First Baptist Church where Brother Dellwood Walker pushed my head down into the cold baptismal: what is it about all our lives men pushing our heads down? He wore duck hunting waders under the white robe. I could see the little hexes on the floor from his bootsoles and thought of Daddy, all the great lost world—the congregation's eyes wide on my rebirth. The organist looked at me goggle-eyed, about to pump the pedals.

Strange to think of it now, Jesus, I mean. That the central act of the world's central religion is all about a virgin getting knocked up without consent, then death and mutilation—total human sacrifice. Sundays at First Baptist, Brother Dell'd summon the deacons who carried trays of grape juice, little shot glasses filled with bitter drink. Then came the trays of saltine crackers. I don't know, maybe it's a meal you're not supposed to like, one that should make you gag a little when it goes down. *Take this, my blood, take this my body*—transubstantiation, Joey calls it, but the whole mess seems pure-D cannibal to me. Give me some space here, let me go. Because Brother Del baptized me with all those blank faces out beyond the baptismal glass. Some fine day, I remember thinking, his scrunched up face looking down at me. Why is it men get such a kick out of holding you down, their eyes locked on yours, waiting for you to give. *Forgive me all this.* My mind then: the house that burned to the ground, my wedding dress, the one Dee'd bought for me with O.W., the lace I wore that day in front of the big glass window that overlooked the crook of river, Joey standing between me and my groom. I remember how light looked through the veil, the gauzy blue sky, how Joey said *I do, I do take this woman*, sweet boy. I picture it burning, the fine ash no eye will ever see.

Jimmy put a red push-point through this exact spot in his map of the world—the center of our lives: Lonoke, Arkansas—where we moved after the house burned and we got Jesus. Spring came—I'm sure it did. Forsythia bloomed. I missed a period, then another. My hair turned. O.W.? The piece of ceiling that fell on his chest maybe burned some sense into his heart; he got Jesus too and ended his career as a Greyhound charter-bus driver and horse track gambler. He got on with Monarch boats in Pine Bluff, hauling these glittery cabin cruisers out west. Joey got taken with him once, so I pictured the two of them flying along the desert highway with three sparkling boats stacked piggy-back.

Jimmy was in speech therapy and first grade then. One perfect autumn day I watched him walk the length of gravel driveway up to the mailbox with its silly little red flag up, where the school bus stopped. A light frost had fallen. He stood out there with the light breath rising. I was looking out the window and could see the sun in his face, how he stood there with his little Snoopy lunchbox, waiting to go where teacher would try so hard to unlock the words from his mouth—and what then? What would come out when the words were unlocked? Would his words remember the forgetfulness of their former lives, the way birds remember routes flown by ancestors? He turned and saw me in the window, this big crooked grin and breath rising and the new sun in autumn that I was pregnant for the third time. He held up sign language for I love you, stood there grinning with his fingers splayed—my blue-eyed son. What words would he remember? Then the bus came and he stepped up and disappeared into the huge curve that cars were always missing, so they'd end up out in the pasture by the little red barn where the swaybacked Palomino chewed grass to the root.

I've got this picture of myself when I first considered adultery. My job was at the Maybelline Factory down I-40 between Sardis and Galloway Exit. I worked day shift on the lipstick line, shoulder to shoulder with three-hundred other women and a few men, all of us stuffing Electric Pink or Cool Peach or Aristotle Red lipsticks into plastic molds. Mornings, I'd wake sleepy-head Jimbo, and Joey'd make Daddy longlegs toast while I drove Trace to Feed My Sheep, the daycare Brother Dell's straight-banged wife ran, always laughing out loud, saying *beans* after every sentence. Then I'd take 89 out into the country, a nice drive with sun raining down on the bitterweed and does crossing the road with yearling fawns—the ripe world all heartbreak-fresh and sweet. I'd park beside the Furlow Methodist Church and wait for the white van to roll up and die. Joey was sixteen then and had this yellow Pinto he'd bought himself with summer construction money. So I'd be sitting there in my oldest son's Pinto, rolling the day over in my head and listening to whatever band of long-haired hippies in his eight track—Z.Z. Top this one day, feisty Texas blues, music with some zing to it. This would be late fall, a payday Friday, maybe. How I latch on to that time, when I was thirty-six, about to be thirty-seven, and O.W.'s off deadheading across Georgia with my picture taped up in the cab of his sleeper. Late fall, hoarfrost on the ground and sugar maple leaves are floating down in tight little zigzags from the tree where newlyweds were photographed. And I'm thinking of the times I said *yes*, how outright weird it was to get married—*to plight one's troth*. And the sugar maple leaves are zigzagging down when the carpool van rolls up, dies, waits for the rest of us to show up, get in, and have ourselves driven to Maybelline to stuff lipsticks all day long with a fifteen minute cigarette break and a baloney sandwich.

Only this day I always picture, I'm listening to this long-beard blues band sing about *tush*, and it's the sort of Arkansas-crisp morning at the tail end of October and I'm thirty-six, no-way over the hill, and the systemic lupus is still just a little firecracker with its fuse on fire in my veins. Over the Pinto's cackly speakers the music thrums, makes me think of Memphis and the river bridge over to Mud Island where they do the Jesus out of the blues all day and all night. Dance to the genuine article, Howlin' Wolf and Carl Perkins' wild twin cousins, Conway Twitty before he died, Jerry Lee, and maybe somebody knock in who'd known Elvis, who'd maybe touched the cuff of my sleeve that time he was in Little Rock before the Central High mess, somebody who could appreciate that I'd caught his eye once, those deep baby blues, and that he'd called me *honey* under his breath and let his lips brush the lobe of my right ear. I'd breathed the essence of the man—a truck driver, for Jesus sake, like O.W., only he could dance. And that voice that made us all love-sick. So my mind has got onto Elvis Presley and I'm not yet thirty-seven, and that one year makes all the difference in the world, believe me. I'm at the edge of a new world, sensing change, maybe, like how you sniff vibrations in the air when a Mack truck is speeding your way, the sun going jack-o-lantern orange on the chrome-dog hood ornament. In the rearview, my face, the *me* I used to be. And Elvis's low voice has got into my head with this hippy music and my heart's beating and my body starts. You see, I love to dance. All my life I've loved to dance, just let go, dance all night, dance a little longer. A frosty morning, the white van and Joey's yellow Pinto the only vehicles in the lot, with that maple putting on a show—Elvis in its sap, in its taproot.

Don't lose this moment, I'm thinking—the *thumpa-thump* in my blood, *one for the money, two for the show*, that's what I'm hearing, how I carry it around in my head. And before I know, I'm outside on the asphalt in front of the Methodist church's newlywed tree, shaking my fanny, maple leaves falling into my hair, dreamy and love-sick. That's how it started, with me kind of spilling out the Pinto door in a groove.

"Go sister," the van driver says out the window and I recognized her straight away, one of the girls I work with, her fingers stained as Aristotle Red as my own, a little pink scar over one eyebrow.

"Honey," I say, "help me," the blues between us.

And for maybe ten minutes by the clock, as the sky brightened, one old jalopy after another rolled up and died and the door opened and another sister got out and shook her booty beneath God and Jesus and the suffering man and all the laughing angels. We danced for the fools we were to have ever said yes, for our children and our children's children, and mamas and daddies and all we'd ever lost or would ever lose, that's how it feels in this picture I carry to my grave. We danced for the world to come.

Must I lose all?

Huffing and puffing, the driver girl helped hoist us up into the white work van, a Chevy with blue vinyl seats that made suck sounds when we moved. Of course, we avoided each other's eyes at all costs for the twenty-five minutes to I-40 and Maybelline, and maybe somebody thought to sing out *oh Maybelline, why can't you be true?* All day long in the big cavern of flourescent light, where we worked in lines surveiled by hidden cameras, one or another of us would go off, let fly with "Hound Dog," or "Jailhouse Rock" or, before it was all over, "Love Me Tender."

We caught fire during the Clinton thing, me and Shawn Terrence. I'd volunteered and somehow ended up in the war room downtown, with James Carville kicking trashcans and all those Arkansas Travelers and F.O.B.'s. It was a wild ride from the start, and somehow my mind got off what had happened to Jimmy, that black hole I'd fallen into. Me and Shawn hooked up for not the first time on election night at the Old Statehouse downtown in Little Rock, just across from the Excelsior with its glass elevator overlooking the Arkansas River. It had been a good, good day. And the fireworks that night, how they burst over the river bridge and me and Shawn and a few of the Travelers smoked a Cuban cigar with Bill himself. Out on the Statehouse lawn about a million Arkansawyers were making a joyful noise, having this party I just can't forget. One hellacious time, for sure, I'm fading now. The endless singing and hugging and kissing—our pure-D jubilation. Somebody from the Democrat-Gazette took my picture in front of the Old State House and the silly thing got printed from here to the moon and back; me in red, holding a thumb with the crazed crowd behind me, the shot catching Shawn in a white shirt and tie, clapping his hands so he looks caught in prayer. The photo was printed in London, Paris, and Rocky Mount, North Carolina. I called O.W. through IceLand Dispatch, and they put me through to the docks in Winston-Salem where he was delivering.

"We're winning honey. We're going to win!"

"I saw your picture," O.W. said, "It's loud there. Are people drunk?"

"I said we're going to win!"

"I said are people *drunk?*"

For some reason I pictured him sitting in the cab of his truck, the smell of aftershave and diesel, a day's stubble on his face, somebody on the CB radio calling for Roadrunner. Truckstop prostitutes would be knocking door to door. All the bad coffee in the world. Burned up brake dust in the air. I was sad for him, that he was no more a part of my world that second than the man in the moon. And even still, I loved him. Have a baby with somebody, two, tell me you don't feel that flesh between you. It's not like a water faucet, turn love on and off. "You'd know what drunk people sound like." I said it.

"Don't fuck him. You know the deal."

"Do what?"

"Don't fuck him. You know the deal."

"Christ, O.W."

"You know the deal."

And that was that—I *did* know the deal. O.W. knew—he had to know. I'm not that careful. And of course he'd threatened more than once to take my life—with a gun, with a knife, with his own bare hands. It'd be a fight, we both knew that.

But I danced all night and night became day. Shawn and I slept till three, him in those silky red underwear. Shawn on the king bed with that smile and bright blue eyes. Shawn Terrence Lord in a tuxedo shirt tucked into faded jeans at *Jacques and Suzanne*'s where we sipped Zellar Swartz Katz and laughed at the Spirit of Arkansas blowing stacks all down the river. The last picture, the one I see so clearly now, is of me and Shawn dressed for the gala, posed by a crystal chandelier. He's a head taller than me. This is our second day in D.C., the inauguration's day after tomorrow. Joey will join us soon. He'll tell Shawn that O.W.'d cut his throat should he ever find out—true enough. Then Bill Clinton will get sworn in and Miller Williams will read the long, wacky poem he wrote half-snockered on bourbon and branch water. Shawn Terrence will turn his face from the camera. He won't allow Joey to photograph him, and I'll be surprised how that hurts, though it seems a smart thing now. He'll write me a long letter, one that explains how it's time to move on to the next horizon, how you had to turn loose of the old before new growth could happen. He'd write something about not mistaking the journey for the destination, wacky California crap if you ask me. And that'll be that. He'll write this long letter that's folded this second in my briefcase, tied with a piece of Traceleen's red school yarn.

10. Joey

One trick I learned from O.W.—leave early. Hit the road at sunrise with your wife and daughter conked out in the backseat. Drive a hundred miles before anybody knows what's hit them. A man-of-war is docked on Mobile Bay, a big, quiet ship with the hull painted gray to make it invisible to enemies at sea. We're about to leave the gulf for good, head up into Mississippi toward Hattiesburg and Jackson and the river bridge between Greenville and Lake Village, Arkansas. The water's slack, low tide, an overcast day. My knuckles ache—this could all go very wrong. I could really fuck things up. Mama, you're dead. I'm mad as hell at you for dying like this. How on earth could you die like this? Us at a goddamn birthday party. Just too goddamn much, these Stepwell theatrics. Outside, big birds glide down close to the water and disappear. The ocean at sunrise is peaceful as Jesus, it makes me want to be home, pruning suckers off the tomato plants in Utah with the dew on the grass and hummingbirds buzzing the yellow blooms.

On the radio—"Hardheaded Woman." Mama involved me with her other men from the word go. Hell fire, I was one of them, wasn't I? Buddy Washer, my blood father out in Arizona, I remember Mama telling me how deeply he'd loved us before he died, before the big accident she invented. She threw away everything she had related to him except me. Now Mama'll never know that I've actually talked to the man, looked his name up in the Tucson directory and listened to him lie at length.

"I love you," he'd said once before we hung up. Then he mailed a ceramic Indian with its ass end stuffed full of skunk weed. What on earth kind of I love you's that? Say?

Then came O.W., me and him all of a sudden dressed in the same spit-shined shoes and clip-on ties, saying I do, I do with the whole goddamn green world spread out thirteen floors down from Grandma Dee's Himalaya House apartment window. You could see the Little Rock Zoo from that window, the dorky little train circling the duck pond, bells ringing. Tugboats butted up against barges on the Arkansas River, thin smoke curling from their engines. "Hauling toilet paper," Grandpa Stepwell told me once on the way out I-40 to the duck woods. "Enough for every shitass from here to New Orleans." Stepwells are like that, liable to say any old thing. Like me saying *I do* at Mama and O.W.'s wedding. Freudian as all get out, every boy wishes to marry the mother who'll do for him what no mother has ever done. The truth is, I was afraid of O.W. from the first time I saw him, his name stitched in red letters over his heart. He adopted me, sure. We learned to live with each other, deer hunt, pitch horseshoes out in the backyard, fill fifty-five gallon drums full of scrap and burn the Jesus out of some trash. He carved a soap box derby car for me during Webelo Roundup. Once I had a fistfight with a guy named Ricky O'Neal in our backyard and some way or another lost my shoes. *Thwack* one went against the bedroom wall when O.W. hauled off and threw them, ashamed I hadn't kicked O'Neal's ass. *Thwack* the other went. He didn't exactly call me a *woodpussy* then, but I could see it in his blue-blue eyes. *You're a woodpussy*, his eyes said. *Woodpussy*, it was written all over his face.

I barely remember this other guy who proposed to Mama while O.W. was in jail, the one who bought a love seat and took me and Melody Dorty fishing down a road where signs kept saying *Beware of Ice* or *Beware Ahead*. Mama'd called me on the phone from Dr. Conn's office. "He's asked me to marry him. Should I?"

"No," I said. "No, no, no."

"Okey-dokey," Mama told me. "If you're sure."

"Mama," I said. "In the whole history of the universe, no mother's ever asked her son if she could get married."

"Well, I just did."

"Well, hell no," I said. How fucked up could things get?

Up front, Shawn Terrence Lord gave me a sick feeling in the stomach. How he turned his back to me and left Mama standing there by herself on Capitol

Hill, just a skinny man with a shag haircut standing with his back to the camera, dumb seagulls landing on the frozen reflecting pool. Mama kept pictures of him in the briefcase by her bed. I saw them once, on a quick trip to Lonoke after she'd taken to the couch with her lupus full flare. She'd summoned me and Renee from Utah, certain she was dying. We slept two nights back in her bedroom and the briefcase was sort of propped up on one end beside her night stand, threatening to pop open before I ever touched it. *Josephine Stepwell Harvell*, I remember thinking that's her name, Mama's, engraved on fake gold. Inside were pictures and letters, twenty-year-old corsages and a piece of Jimmy's umbilical cord in an envelope marked HOLY.

An entire roll of Kodak—*our royal paper behind your best memories*—is dedicated to Ocho Rios, the trip Mama was supposed to take with Floy and Juanita Waymack from First Baptist, only there's Shawn Terrance sipping a banana drink in a red speedo. He's grown a moustache. Love buoys life. A briefcase with a flimsy combination lock any fingernail file could pop. And Shawn.

I recall one photo of Mama alone, smiling, happy in an Ocho Rios beach chair, the strong light getting her in the eyes.

Renee's up by Gulfport. We switch and she points the Pathfinder north on Highway 49, up through the DeSoto National Forest, land Dirky Lee inherited when his own mama hemorrhaged and died on an operating table with him looking right down on her through the glass. I always felt for him over that, maybe it's even one of the reasons we were friends; what a terrible thing, I always thought, lose your mother like that. She signed him over ten-thousand acres of Mississippi hardwood. He'd have these periodic clear cuts done in the DeSoto National Forest, so he was always about half loaded. Dirky paid for excursions to the *Jeannie's Drive-Through Bare Naked Car Wash*, and bar tabs at Roger's on Dickson Street in Fayetteville. Too bad about him stealing Jimmy's funeral. I have Renee stop at the gates of the University of Southern Mississippi, where he's from, where his old man was college Dean or some such bullshit. My piss is bright yellow, I'm not drinking enough water.

By Greenville, I'm behind the wheel again. The river bridge from Mississippi to the Arkansas side is a low steel affair, all business and reason, nothing at all like the pretty cabled-up version upriver in Memphis. I cross over in the deep afternoon with the sun in my face—straight up happy hour. My native state.

Arkansas, the word breaks into three hard pieces when you say it.

My mouth is salty, I don't know why.

The sign says, *Welcome To Arkansas: Land of Opportunity.*

Me and Mama, we crossed here once on the way down to Jacksonville, Florida. A relation had lost a child, a baby boy. I've forgotten its name, but this child had died, had in fact drowned in a bathtub, of all places. He'd been bathing with his four-year-old brother who'd left him alone for a few minutes to check out the ice cream truck outside. As a kid, I pictured him hearing loud music from a warped speaker howling all down the street—that's how I always saw it. The one brother leaving the other in piss-warm water. So this four-year-old leaves his baby brother in the tub, runs out naked to the red-eyed ice cream man with his three notes blaring. Who can say where the rest of all creation was? The little boy whose name won't come slipped down in the bubbly water and he drowned. They dressed him in sailor suit in a little baby casket. Mama and I were living with Dee then, some apartment with a tiny square of yard where I witnessed a mailman get arrested, thrown bucking and screaming into the backseat of a cop car. He'd talked to Mama like he knew her, like he'd come to speak to her personally. This mailman had screamed at Mama. He'd looked at me like he owned me, like I was his property. And then this little boy drowned and the two events somehow twined in my mind. When I hear the ice cream truck in our neighborhood, about the time Lara starts screaming for quarters, I think of them both—the little boy dressed in a sailor suit in a baby casket and the mailman's face, his red lips pressed up against the cop car's rear window.

Mama told me the story on a bus that crossed this same river bridge, bound for sunny Florida, retracing the drive we've just made. My name is Joey Harvell—a Stepwell on my mother's side. I'm an adoptee, a step-son, a half-brother, a father, a husband. I'm good-crazy, mojo-city. Dwarf-blood, humpback genes probably, run through my veins. Santa, my blood father, has a belly full of weed. I'm going home to marry my mama.

Welcome to the Natural State.

The cupola of the Jefferson County Courthouse was shot off by a Confederate cannon during the battle of Pine Bluff, of October 25, 1863, the nearest thing to an outright castration the commanding general could exact on the blue-balled Yankees whose flag had been hung there. I know this because it says so on page 37 of Renee's *Southern Accent: A Collection of Favorite Recipes* by the Junior League of Pine Bluff which has somehow gotten packed in Lara's book bag. The cookbook's signed and dedicated to Renee by the Honorable Congressman Anthony Cleopatra himself, whom she'd interned under after graduating from University of Maryland, and whose district included the grand cupola-less courthouse. In 1906 an addition was made on the rear—a clock and a bell tower were added. My wife's spent a good amount of time around page 37 in the cookbook, the next page being Eggs Sardou, one of our absolute favorites because Renee's a genuine wizard with Hollandaise, switches off between Sardou and Benedict on Christmas mornings, my birthday breakfasts. Which all makes sense as we drift up 65 into Jefferson County, driving off-center into the late afternoon sun, hungry and thirsty with happy hour all but gone. Lara, our issue, cannot know how this town that stinks of paper mill and the unbelievably toxic Pine Bluff Arsenal where live human beings burn nerve gas to this day, is a nexus—a holy omphalos of sorts—between myself and her mother, between our families even, which seems as odd and serendipitous as any story Mama ever told; she'd agree with me on this one, and did so more than once in the company of strangers, once in underground Atlanta at a grill your own steak place, before she got looped on her lupus meds and had to wear those dark glasses.

Today is a Monday—*moonday.* The earth is hauling ass through the Large Magellanic Cloud, four days or so from Summer Solstice when the sun sets straight down the end of our Utah street and we burn wishes on the patio, grill a chicken on fresh sage over charcoal and drink the sweet Jesus out of double vodkas tonic. Renee's missed the Watson Chapel loop, so here we are going straight through town on Dollarway Road. The mill stinks through the air-conditioner vents. I grew up smelling it out of the clear blue when the wind blew out of the southeast, usually around the holidays, when everybody accused everybody else of bean gas. Here's a wide bend in the Arkansas we'll follow the rest of the way home, water come from high in Colorado where you can piss one side to the other. A blues show is coming over some spot way left on the dial, a Little Rock Station—Cab Fare Blues it's called, the DJ a sexy-voiced smoker who plays John Lee Hooker and Howlin' Wolf and Lightnin' Hopkins—men singers Mama loved. They'd made the Arkansas Hall of Music Fame downtown in the Old State House where Bill Clinton announced his candidacy out on that wide veranda, straight away from the Excelsior Hotel with its glass elevator where all that blow job business maybe or maybe didn't go on with that Beebe girl. Across the street sits the grand old Capitol Hotel where anybody with any sense goes to do whatever illicit thing they want.

Lara's asking if we're *there*, she's hungry, she *hates* this truck ride. Why am I so *mean* to her? She starts in with the word Renee and I sling at each other in arguments. From the carseat, my own daughter's screaming *Peckerhead! Peckerhead! Peckerhead!* into my left ear.

She gains moral support when Renee smiles in the rearview.

"Mommy. Daddy is a Peckerhead!"

"Cutey pie. We'll be there soon."

"I'm not a cutey pie," Lara screams. The stolen Pathfinder smells worse with the paper mill blowing through its vents. Crumbs from our road food gather on the floorboard, in the folds of our stale clothes—crackers, peanuts, Cap's stale snack mix.

Renee says, "Look. That courthouse."

True—the razorblade hands on the clock say quarter till six and we've driven since sunrise. On the road, I always think of O.W. For my wedding, he gave me his gold plated pocket watch: for O.W. Harvell from IceLand for 1,000,000 safe driving miles, it says. A million miles—from here to the moon and back and more. So much time alone to sort the future from the past, to devise lists of events necessary for changing the course of either. Sometimes, when he drove on black ice or through tornadoes, Mama'd have us all clasp hands at the supper table and pray while our Tony's Pizza got cold. Amen, she'd say, and Jimmy'd get echolalia and his chin would lock up.

Aretha Franklin belts out "Respect Yourself." Renee catches the refrain, sings. They both have hazel eyes, Lara and Renee—a trait they've inherited from Meg Rockerson, who was a West Virginia Showalter and Vice-President of the secret sorority of Delphina at WVU.

Renee makes a right into a Phillips 66 and takes Lara to potty. Gasoline leaks on my sandal while I fill up and I feel like I have no business whatsoever here, a fool boy from a family who burned wood fence for cooking, on the way to his mother's casket, that's how I'm feeling. Still, we don't eat, drive north, each mile heavier than the last.

"You okay, Joe? Are you going to be okay?"

This is a crooked, crooked life. "Yeah," I say. "Right as rain."

Monarch Boat Factory is built on Lake Pine Bluff—a sprawling military-industrial looking place with high fences and a central check-in point for drive-thrus. Just now a guy in uniform stands looking like he's about to salute or shoot a trespasser without hesitation—one or the other. This is the place O.W. drove for all those years after the house fire, when we'd moved up to Lonoke where he and Mama got Jesus. He'd blow his air horn at the end of Willy Ray, and come driving up with cabin cruisers stacked on metal racks, flattening out the trailer's natural arc. Big glittering boats bound for California from Pine Bluff with its stinking mill and arsenal and castrated courthouse.

O.W. was driving for Monarch—hauling piggyback boats—the summer he sort of kidnapped me, and I first saw the west—the first time I'd remember it, anyway—from the cab of his Peterbilt. I kept up with the states we entered and departed by sticking state stickers from the truck stops on a green suitcase with my mother's smell on it. I'd wonder about her and Jimmy and baby Traceleen, look up at the Milky Way and feel like I was drifting into pieces, little islands of myself coming apart. Then in the dark, I'd watch the midget television up under the dash, and think about the way O.W. did things, how he chewed food and forged his log books and farted while he pissed. His every move alien to me as the dusty Wyoming mesas where, at any moment, a hoof or an ear would twitch and there would appear a herd of antelope shining where before had been nothing at all.

Outside Rawlins, not far from the Big Sky State Prison, O.W. claimed to know a place where gravity ceased to exist. He pulled off roadside, where he was all the time swerving at eighty miles an hour, laying into the air horn and scaring roadside hippies shitless in their sleeping bags. "Which way's uphill?" he asked. "This way or that?"

We faced a valley where I could see the State Pen, men walking on hard concrete behind fences inside of fences—a real prison like I'd never seen before. "Back that way," I said. I jerked my thumb back toward the sleeper where a pretty picture of Mama, one from before the fire, was Scotch taped to the ceiling. "That way's up," I said and pointed behind us. "We're going downhill."

"Back that-away, huh? Behind us is up, right?"

"Yeah, behind us is up.'"

He slipped the huge black gear shifter knob into neutral, halting all those gear boxes in their grease, took his polished black boots off the clutch and brakes, took both hands off the wheel. Air from the brakes hissed beneath us. It was May, hot as Hades in Arkansas, but a freaky snow had fallen out here in Wyoming and we were in tee-shirts. For about a hundred fifty miles since Cheyenne we'd trailed a Kenworth rig hauling a brand new Tilt-O-Whirl. Like I said, it was morning and the sun was rising up behind our backs, shining off the new snow and into all those mirrors on the Tilt-O-Whirl. This carney ride was a cousin or brother maybe to the one that had hurled me and Jimmy over the sawdust at the Lonoke County Fair while Mama watched us and talked to the one-armed barker at the Rifle Bullseye Shoot. And now, out in the wild West—kidnapped, maybe, to blackmail my mother into taking him back—all the license plates had pictures of a cowboy riding a bucking horse. All this on the roadside with home behind my back, O.W. in neutral—life could go either way.

The truck creaked, shivered on its wheels for a few seconds. Then it started to roll uphill, complaining like it hurt. Just a slight movement at first—the sensation of going backwards, the patterns of light and dark shifting. Nothing much, I was a kid in a big truck that reeked of the six states in between me and Mama, Jimmy and Traceleen, our half-beagle Suzi-Q. A smidgen of movement, the wheels creaking under the heavy boats and the airbrakes hissing.

O.W. got this look on his face, part feigned surprise, but something else, too. "Which way's down, Joe. Show me down."

Miles west now, falling away in the direction that my mind told me was down, the Tilt-O-Whirl glared over a ridge of pure white, then disappeared. We were moving upward, that much I knew, thirty tons in tow. Maybe gravity *had* quit for him? I was a country kid—what'd I know? Blue sage on the sunny side of Highway 80 had got free of a snow drift—how it shined. And the moment the truck rolled uphill seemed somehow connected to my whole life; I knew that if I understood this, the rest would all make sense some day. Here was my test. The moment was nigh. There in Wyoming—a chance to get the truth straight from the horse's mouth. Another semi blew by, shook us like big waves. Life with Mama and O.W. had been a wild ride, a real whirl up until then. What did I know about the fundamental laws of physics and the universe, Newton's gravity, the way space binds unlike objects? We were rolling faster know, hauling ass backwards uphill.

"Am I kidnapped, O.W.?"

"I ast you which way's down."

"Tell me if I'm kidnapped."

"Don't be a idiot. How can a daddy kidnap his own boy? Looky out there."

We rolled uphill. The moon was out. I saw its pale curve, jagged mountains way off and thought of Mama rocking powder-blue Traceleen. Back home, the power was off—they were reduced to burning wood fence. I said, "It's a trick."

"Trick? You sure?" O.W. raised his brows.

"Yeah," I lied. Up was down and down was up, that's how it seemed. The prison's razor wire made curlicues where men walked cautiously in blaze orange suits.

In the dream that reinvents itself as I grow older, objects—workboots, my daughter's blue rattle—receive a power all their own and ghost dance across the bedroom floor. I'm always paralyzed, unable to scream even, and I wake with Renee's hands on my face. "It's okay," she says. "You're dreaming. Jesus, Joey." And of course I'd learn the truth, how downhill and uphill got switched out west—the light and distance and elevation was a mirage all trucker's knew about, so many'd stopped in the Rawlins Rip Griffin Truck Stop to have their transmissions torn apart for nothing. Everyone knew about how downhill was uphill outside of Rawlins, Wyoming. But for that half-mile, and a shitload of years after, O.W. seemed to undo gravity.

"You sure?" O.W.'d asked.

Almost to the summit, the diesel hauled ass, its engine highptiched as the first keen a mother makes for her new-dead son. And in the valley below, shaved-headed prisoners walked circles upon circles behind razor wire. I saw myself as two—the one I am, and the one I'd left behind. Only, in the dream the two are one, the still-born truth concealed in its heart. We made for the top. Our air brakes hissed and the boats glittered and new-fallen snow shined for a million miles across Wyoming to the sea.

11. Josephine

My flinch is pure instinct, the way a hand gets thrown up in front of a man-high fire, only it's no shield. O.W. shines the photo in my face. We lock eyes. *Till death do you part*, the preacher'd said, all those years ago when Joey, the son from my first mistake in wedlock, stood between us as best man, dressed like O.W.'s twin. He's supposed to be deadheading across Tennessee, O.W., bound for Rocky Mount and ten tons of slaughter turkey, instead of standing here beside the Jacuzzi, swiping steam with a snapshot of Shawn Terrence Lord, my one-time lover. Half a bank statement shines in his front pocket—so he knows the score there, too.

"Where's pretty boy now?" He says it through shut teeth.

The sentence settles between us. And before I can talk it happens. He's threatened a thousand times, and we've gone at each other's throats more than once. I laid him open cheek to chin with a fingernail on the night I screamed for Joey to get help. I've kissed his tears, wiped his blood. Now, through the bubbles of my breath, his blue eyes sear. But here in Jimmy's room?—surely to God he can't do it in Jimmy's room.

Seen from underwater, everything gets bigger.

The photo's from Ocho Rios ten years ago, the trip I lied a three-way alibi into, and even had a photograph doctored to show me, Floy Melton and Juanita standing on the whitest sand, all that blue ocean eyeballing us every which way. We've had a *time*—me and Shawn Terrence—tromping through waterfalls and snorkeling up fish, gorging ourselves on smoked conk. It's hot as Hades, the kind of heat you forget. Shawn's scotch-happy. He's singing "Earth Angel," hanging the high notes out to dry. We're waiting for the rest of our lives. Shawn's got these big deer eyes. When I take his picture, one goes red and the other silver. He smiles like there's no such thing as O.W. on this earth, like nice teeth and muscle and heart can get you through. *Good god*, I thought, that lightness you get in your blood. *No, no, no, no, no*—not love. Of a sudden, like when you walk out the back door after an all-night snow and the forsythia bloomed. Sun shines through the petal veins and a man touches you from behind, kisses your neck, maybe, and then you trip on a patio chair and break teeth. That's how it's always been for me—*love*—stricken like every other idiot breathing air.

After, Shawn Terrence flew off to L.A. and joined A.A., and I saved every scrap of him I could find. This second, he's in the briefcase beside my night stand—the one with the *oh so flimsy lock* that a duck could pick it with its beak.

My hot tub's in Jimmy's room, the son me and O.W. lost in a car wreck sixteen years ago. Except for the therapy tub, everything's the same, dusty with spiderwebs high in the corners, but the same. Like Jimmy could walk in the door any second, six-feet tall with sawdust in his hair, and we'd all hug each other. The nightmare'd be undone and we could live our lives in love again. O.W.'s crouched over me. His flattop's cut high and tight. The wedding ring I bought him from M.M. Conn's in Little Rock shines on a finger beside Shawn Terrence. He's seen all the rest, we both know that. Like I couldn't tell all the times he's rifled my briefcase, then tried to leave it ramshackle the way I keep things. There's great order in my disorder.

I could scream bloody murder.

Dora's next door in her kitchen, ogling Gomez on *One Life to Live*, waiting for anything at all to let her know she's alive. One scream from me and Dora'd speed-dial the law, then run over here slinging a dead king snake and curses for withered testicles and whatnot. Dora's a hoot—she'd save my ass.

Trouble is—I'm supposed to be dead already. That was the deal. Two months ago I was cut open to remove the mass in my chest, just under my breast bone—scar tissue from who knows. Like Stepwells go through life accumulating scar tissue where their hearts should be.

"With your lupus," Dr. Casket said, "anesthesia's going to be tricky. Get your ducks in a row, Josie."

"Doctor," I said, "Why are you named Casket?"

"My name?"

"Yeah."

"Come again?"

"What kind of idiot lets themselves get cut on by somebody named Casket?" That's what Daddy taught me—stay on the sunny side, slay'em with laughter.

"Oh, gotcha" he said. "I knew this gastrointestinal guy named Shitz. He's all the time saying, "'Ain't this the shits? Ain't that the shits?'"

O.W. was in the room—the TV humming. He heard what Casket had to say. And that very afternoon, two weeks before the surgery, we drove to Jim Ed Brown Men's on Cantrell, where I made him try on two dozen-suits before choosing the deep blue one that made him look like the man I met in the bread aisle at Tabor's grocery. Then he drove me to Ballou's Boutique in the Heights where I picked out what I'd wear for the viewing, real unusual— outfitting yourself for *those* eyes. That was April—two months ago, and I'd just deposited twenty-thousand buckeroos into Lonoke Bank & Trust—disability insurance. It was a boatload of money, more than we'd ever had at once—me and O.W.—and before I could get his name scratched off the account he'd gone out and bought a four-wheeler and new set of dentures, Ping golf clubs, a knife set, a beard trimmer. One morning while wheeling me into Waffle House, he mumbled something about a Cadillac Seville.

"O.W.," I said. "You don't wear a beard. What's with the trimmer?"

"I take care of you," was what he said. And he had a point—I was invalid. Have I said I'm invalid? Does that matter in the least at times like this?

"Nobody drives Cadillacs anymore."

My wheelchair banged the glass door. "Uh-uh, Josephine," he said. "Not after all I've stood." And that was that—case closed. Then came the operation, and I was honestly supposed to die. I believed it in my heart's heart, enough to draft a longhand will. I made pallbearer lists and wrote out the words to the songs my people'd sing in Sanctuary Hall of First Baptist: "I'll Fly Away," and "Pow'r in the Blood," and "Angel Flying Too Close to the Ground." I asked Joey to deliver my eulogy—to put some *umph* into it. He's the son left standing, only from Buddy, a man I loved in Arizona who just happens to be the biggest liar in the world.

Of course, the will never saw an attorney—Stepwells aren't *attorney* kind of people. Dense as gumbo, but we've got good hearts—nobody says a word about our hearts.

We planned everything out, my service, how Joey'd speak the eulogy for the family, and what peckerhead Brother Dell was allowed and not allowed to say. We talked through who got what. I read my husband my will, a love letter really, and O.W. sat their nodding. He's not a word man. But he was sweet, even cried some when I got to his part. By the time Dr. Casket cut me open, my ducks were in a row. I was ready, save the briefcase left leaning beside my night stand. That's how the world stood before they put me under.

Only, I didn't die.

Dr. Casket met me in recovery with a big smile on his face. "You're going to make it, honey. Honey? You're going to live, Josephine Stepwell. Ain't that the shits? You're alive."

Beside me, O.W. nodded. But he wasn't looking at me, more like some me laying beside me. Joey says he got real wacky on the phone, that he'd call up and say the most amazing things in a funny voice. He'd pretend he'd called earlier, forget whole conversations. I didn't know why. Who knows a damn thing about men, really? Their crooked insides? What they're capable of dreaming up in an eighteen-wheeler dragging dead birds across Tennessee?

The hell of it—not only did I not die, I got better. Better and better and better. Dora'd call at three a.m. She had the dirt on Brother Dell and Deacon Meloy—we'd be in stitches till the sun came up. For the first time in sixteen years my lupus went into full remission. The swelling went down in my knees so walking didn't kill me. Honeysuckle bloomed all May and songbirds went crazy for every sunrise, or so it seemed. I kept thinking, I *am* alive. I am *alive*. What do you do when you think you're about to die but don't? Say?

I planted an herb garden, sage and basil and catnip. Joey and I set a family reunion up at Heber for Fourth of July. Every morning—O.W. out on his run—I'd throw open the doors and go outside without my dark glasses. Horses would neigh in the lime field and I'd brew tea and fry bacon. I added oregano, chives, cherry tomato. Sometimes I'd turn on the radio and stand swaying in the doorway, neither inside nor outside. I smoked cigarettes and drank sweet wine when O.W. was on his run. I wrote Shawn Terrence one letter, then another. And he wrote me back. And he wrote me back again.

But honey, it takes a long time, drowning. Mine's taken a lifetime. I was born Stepwell, landed gentry on the Trail of Tears. Uncle Marlin was Yell County Sheriff. Famous for stealing elections, he'd once ridden on the back of a live jackass right into the fully convened Arkansas State Legislature. Beryl, Jeryl and Meryl'd all passed through the University up in Fayetteville. They'd played tennis with the Fulbright boys. Charles Rickey was an expert on spiders. Dodger'd punted for the Razorbacks. Uncle Waylow was a pulpwood man, balling his own diesel down Danville Mountain. My paternal grandfather owned a hotel. Grandma Ida traced our line to John and John Quincy Adams. Aunt Naveen counts Jesse James among our kin. And Daddy was the apple of their eyes—cream of the Stepwell crop. I picture how it must've been for Mama, all swallowed by his letter jacket, Marion Weldon Stepwell stitched inside the left-hand pocket.

He cut firewood on the side, split seasoned oak in rickets and cords up against the back wall of Tri-County hunt club—and this made money so Dee let it slide. I see the two of us the day ambulance slammed up.

"Get in, both of you," Doc Jenkins, a cousin on one side, screamed. He reached a big, palsied hand out the door and hauled us in. The ambulance took off with such a jolt we all three fell on the metal gurney.

It had a chill to it, the sort of cold that stays.

The road up Chickalah Mountain was like running your tongue over missing teeth, the truck slip-sliding through fresh mud. There'd been an accident with the bucksaw, Doc said.

Weldon was up there. And another man. The call'd come from the hunt club. He'd cut a leg off, was hemorrhaging.

The girl shouldn't see this.

When the doors opened, a calm came over my mama, the way it did when she prayed out loud in public, that look in her eye. He was pale and bleeding to death, the second leg cut half through as well. She ripped the hem off her dress, twisted a tourniquet beneath the knee, what was once a knee. Fine blood misted our faces.

We twisted and loosened the tourniquet all the way to St. Mary's in Russellville–
an hour drive. The sun was out, rain falling in silver bullets. *The devil beating*
his wife, people called it. A hundred or more stood waiting on the hospital lawn
when the ambulance wailed up. Half the Littlejohn baseball team was there, as was
Coach, who'd lost a son to sniper fire in France, and whose wife, a nurse, was the
first to see the scene inside the ambulance.

"*Dear God*," she'd screamed. The hospital's double doors opened and, right
there in front of us this woman stripped naked, wrapped herself in a sheet, and
disappeared into the operating room for the emergency surgery that followed.

Flowers had bloomed. The war was over, this should be a happy time. We'd
got him to the hospital before he bled to death. There was *hope*. Anything could
happen. I come from a people who believe.

Later, a voice hollered from the stone balcony, "*He'll live!*"

Somebody yelled "*Praise Jesus*," and eyes filled with tears of joy.

Before Christmas he'd be hooked on morphine. But that night my people
made a joyful noise on the hospital lawn, until it got too late for such and the
jubilation passed.

I can't be sure of it at all, but I was there once. At Tri-County, I believe. Surely I was
there before he cut his leg off. The night is pitch black and we're on that road out past
Wonderview High School, where Daddy'd played basketball his senior year. The stars
just blaze, no moon to light the gravel roads Daddy navigates by heart. He was born
out there on Stepwell land, the Trail of Tears where Cherokee had walked and wept,
it was in his blood and bone. Daddy's headlights reflect back at us in the red eyes of
animals. We were quiet, I don't know what had happened, but him and Dee'd just
had a knock-down-drag-out. He'd hit her in the head with a peanut butter jar—I
don't know why. And now I was in Daddy's truck, in my sunflower pajamas, five
or six maybe, riding into the Solgahatchia bottom where an old rickety monument
mars the Trail of Tears—right down the middle of Stepwell land. Out past Saint
Vincent's Catholic, and past the invisible line where electricity stops and people still
burn for light. We drove past boundaries out Tri-County road with its steel bridge
missing boards so silver water shone through.

An owl swung down into the beams of Daddy's bright lights, maybe a barn owl or a Great Western—I don't know—but there it was and Daddy hit it.

"Goddamnit," Daddy said. "Fuck everything."

He got out and I heard the thing thud in the truck bed, and then we went off down the dark road with a just-dead owl quivering in the bed behind us. Some Indians believe owls are messengers that forecast real bad luck about to happen. Others point out how they see through the darkest dark and hardly ever miss their prey—fearsome hunters, owls. Country folk claim that the owl sees the truth stillborn and pure, no living thing can lie to the owl. Either way, the owl's strong mojo, though all that was beyond me then, a girl in sunflower pajamas, riding with my daddy in the Solgahatchia bottom.

Mens faces were lit up around a fire when we drove up. When the dream comes on nights when I'm alone, the sparks rise up in rivulets, loopy figures like crows flying eights into updraft thermals. One man's face shines. He throws a log and the fire gets man-high, all those crazy sparks.

"Mornin' or is it evenin'," the fire-man says. "Come have one."

Daddy gets out and stands by the fire. A bottle is passed. Dogs lope outside the ring of fire, the flames licking their eyes. Everybody seems happy, their mouths gape open. Teeth show. They move around the circle to where Daddy stands, where he starts talking. The story is the old one, the tale that draws men out to hunt clubs and duck shacks and county-line honkeytonks from DesArc to Carthage, the old, old story of bloodletting and initiation, how it is to be a man. Wild as neolithics, men're born for hunt and slaughter in woods that wives and children must not enter. This African man I met in the campaign, he told me how when he was sixteen he'd once stood in a ritual circle, allowed an elder to cut off the tip-end of his penis. Jesus, men. How they fuck themselves out of the grave. The price for such is heavy. The real law of men is words once only uttered in gut, sinew and fist—the flashing teeth, action and reaction; man is animal and animal commits no wrong. Isn't that how it goes? Freedoms are either abandoned or carried out in secret places like Tri-County Coon Club, out in the dark where bottles pass and the fire's stoked and the ancestral circle is rejoined in the season of blood sport. The truth before truth was called truth. I gazed on them as if staring into a den where rattlesnakes dance upright—the firelight on their faces, their voices mingling with night noises. I don't know how long, maybe this all a dream, and I was only a girl sleeping, dreaming of a man like my daddy among men by a fire near the mouth of the deep, dark wood. Maybe I was dozing when the noise started, the high shrieks rising louder and louder, so I was afraid the owl had come back to life, all of us infected with owl mojo for the rest of our lives.

It was, of course, a woman. She shook her head the way women with long hair have of shaking their heads, and I could see both white breasts and the light on her face. The truck door was open on Daddy's side. I could hear all of it. Maybe that woman out there by the fire, whose face was like a girl's face, maybe she screamed out for help, so far back in the woods that no ear on earth would ever hear. Maybe she pleaded for mercy. Who can say? Who would deliver her? Daddy? Some dark God who'd have Abraham lay his own son's sweet neck on the table rock while the sword came down? What on earth could she have been thinking, this girl-woman out on the Trail of Tears at that time of night? What sort of mother would raise her daughter to end up that way? How can such a thing happen? How to explain? *Oh lord of hosts, if I'm not dead yet, please tell me how it can be*? How? Is the dream just a dream? Or maybe, instead of stoppering my ears against those piercing cries, something else?

I soar on owl's wings, bloodstained in the wind, up and up until the man-high fire fades; the blue earth opens its black swan's wings so that no man will ever take me from behind and the girl screaming her fool head off will shush for good and ever and be healed.

Part Two

12. Lonoke, Arkansas

The Super 8's across the road from Knight's Grocery, where I once paid to see LEVIATHAN: SEA MONSTER OF THE DEEP, a gray whale floated in a semi-trailer full of formaldehyde. Behind the check-in counter, a wall clock has *Hari Krishna* written in red across its white face. The Indian owner has never looked me in the eye. I know her by the smell of curry, how it forever leaks from a door behind the front desk, her family's suite entrance. She's taken off her veil since our last visit—the red dot floating between her eyes. "Your father, Mr. Harvell. We have two messages."

Out in the Pathfinder, Renee and Lara sit with the air on high. It's hot as hell, you forget a pain like heat. Asphalt mirages shimmer over the hotel parking lot. Renee's had to pee since Carlisle.

One note, written in the hostesses precise hand says *Joey, Key on top of electric box. Gone to get haircut. Judy and Bold flying down. O.W.* Next is a hand I've seen him write into the IceLand Driver's Log on Sundays after a heavy meal. He'd be about to hit the road—eastbound in an IceLand rig—forging his eight hours on, eight hours off across Tennessee and North Carolina. *Viewing tomorrow afternoon*, O.W.'s written on the Super 8 note pad.

"122," the hostess says. "At government rate. Bottom floor. How many nights?" Children laugh behind the wondrous smelling door.

We've never really talked about anything but extra towels—the Indian hostess and me—but I've watched her children grow from babies, there's something to say for that. "I don't know how long we'll be here."

She passes card keys. "As long as you require. Our ice machine is out." We meet eyes. "We're sorry."

I stick my head out one of the double glass doors, yell 122 to Renee, and point east. Lara's already tumbled from our renegade Pathfinder, joyously swinging open the pool deck gate. A cedar gazebo's been built across the lawn; sun shines through the lattice work.

The hostess lights a stick of incense beneath the Krishna clock, disappears through the family door. She's remembered Mama's state discount, has interacted with O.W. He's stood in this very spot, breathing, the air hissing a little over the front tooth I chipped on the day *Leviathan* came.

Uncle Bold and Aunt Judy drive up while I've got Lara Super 8 poolside, Renee off buying enough vodka to kill a horse. Judy's O.W.'s sister, who years ago exiled herself the hell out of Arkansas for Baltimore, Maryland and a good-hearted Pole named Bold Dujenski. They get out of a silver rental under the check-in awning. Bold recognizes me straight away, waves a big hand as Lara cannonballs off the shallow end ledge. They leave both doors open. For a second it seems a remarkable coincidence—us here at the same time.

Bold says, "We're floored. I'm so sorry, Jimmy."

"Joey." Judy hugs me over the pool fence. She's crying. "We've got to stop meeting like this," she says.

Fifteen years ago they'd walked into the Washington D.C. restaurant where I waited tables to tell me Jimmy'd died. In walked Uncle Bold and Aunt Judy, a lively Friday crowd crowing through the tail end of lunch. Bold said, "Where's the men's room, Jimmy?" Inside, Uncle Bold put a hand on my shoulder. "Your brother's dead," he said. Only he got the names bass-akwards, as he ever had since I'd known him. "Jimmy," he said and looked me straight in the eye. "Joey's dead. He died in a car wreck last night."

Lara drips beside me. Honeysuckle's in the air.

"She's beautiful," Judy says. "Where's Renee?"

"Buying liquor."

"Good," Bold says and shakes out a cigarette.

Judy says, "What's your name, honey?"

Lara giggles behind my back. The sun feels good. "Tell her your name."

She says, "Lara."

"Little lovely Lara."

Judy looks rough, like somebody who's traveled a long way for a funeral.

"Ask the hostess for government rates. She'll know what you're talking about."

Judy hugs me again and this time I smell she's been drinking. "Have you spoken to O.W.?" Bold puts his hand on her shoulder.

"No. I haven't."

Lara and I are eating road food when Renee walks in. We've showered and walked the parking lot perimeter where road-dusty blackberries are going purple. My mouth is salty. I mean to say that my mouth tastes like I've gnawed a salt block all 1077.3 miles from Melbourne Beach, Florida up to Lonoke, all those miles of grit between my teeth. Renee's bought barbecue sandwiches from Mean Pig, and a plastic half-gallon of Popov Vodka.

"Bold and Judy are here."

"Here?"

"Here."

"Where?"

"Out there. They've got a room."

"What did O.W. say?"

"Nothing."

"What?"

"I didn't call yet."

"Well you better." Renee starts unpacking the watery cooler into our mini-fridge. "You should. Right now."

Lara's cartoon is *Power Puff Girls*, these super hero bitches from second grade or something who're beating the Jesus out of some poor bad guy. "Help," he says. "Enough, enough," he cries. Lara screams when I click the TV off, as if I've committed violence.

Renee says, "Hell, Joey."

On a chair outside the front door, out in the humid night, cicadas make that ratchet noise that gets inside your teeth. Across the street, a snowcone vendor does business where *Leviathan* was once parked. A bare bulb shines—I can see his head.

Renee's tired. "Joey," she says through the window. "Call."

How must O.W. have felt fifteen years ago when the dispatchers radioed that Mama was waiting at the terminal. That she was a wreck. That something awful had happened and he needed to skip his remaining drops, get home A.S.A.P. Deadheading across Tennessee through Nashville and Memphis, the glass pyramid reflecting before the river bridge and that long stretch of earth between places. Then Mama had to tell him that Jimmy was dead and he got that look on his face—half surprise, half something else. Jimmy, his blood son's name—how long did that word take to sink in?

I call. Only instead of O.W., it's Mama, her voice on the answering machine, and I don't expect that, not for a second, her sweet voice telling me she can't make it to the phone right now, that if I'll leave my message at the sound of the beep, she'll get back to me soon as she can. Just to hear her, I try again. And again. Until finally her voice is gone, just silence, empty space.

A car drives up across the street and two girls order cones. The vendor'd have enough ice for a zillion vodka tonics—enough to float a whale like the dead grey that lay over there in 1985. This was the Dixie circuit—it was nothing for a Peterbilt to pull off the interstate with a six-hundred pound rat, two-headed goats or Donkey Woman nursing horsey-faced twins. *Leviathan*'s arrival coincided with our fistfight—mine and O.W.'s—the one we had just before Jimmy died. We'd all been driving back from having a family photograph in Little Rock, Trace and Jimmy in the backseat of the blue Cougar, me up front with Mama— O.W. driving. I was twenty-four that summer, living home again from school, barhopping and fighting nights and finishing concrete days. Mama's lupus had just kicked in, barely, just barely. Me and Jimmy'd gone out drinking the night before the scheduled sitting. In Jacksonville, we got pretty shit-faced at a cowboy bar— which was my fault— and danced with Air Force women until two in the morning. O.W.'d smelled it on my breath. He'd glowered all morning and I'd glowered back. I was serious about not taking any guff from anybody by then, especially O.W. Earlier that fall, Sophomore year at the U of A, after I'd been arrested for DWI, he showed up out of the blue to take my car away. On my desk he found a copy of a Chinese folk tale book named *Monkey*. He'd jabbed a hard finger at the cover where this picture of a monkey had *Monkey* written in big black letters across its head.

"That's about evolution, isn't it?"

Before I could say no, that it was about these Chinese people who were poor fucks and lived on the hard earth just like us, O.W. threw *Monkey* across my desk, took the keys to my blue Cutlass and drove off down Highway 71 to Lonoke, without saying *goodbye* or *kiss my ass* or *your mama's worried about you*, or anything at all. Maybe I felt sorry for myself. Did he remember the railroad tracks, how his head bled all down the back of his white shirt—the one with O.W. written on the heart side of his chest? Fuck him.

The Cougar had power windows and I'd rolled mine down. O.W. rolled it up. "The air's on," he said.

"I want fresh air."

"Tough," he said.

I said, "Fuck you, O.W."

He let the car coast onto the highway curb. "*Joey*," Mama said.

"Do *what*?" O.W. said.

"St-st-stop this," Jimmy said. Traceleen sat white-faced.

"I said fuck you. Fuck you, O.W. Hey Jimmy? Trace? Anybody ever tell you about how I lay in bed one night listening to him beat Mama. She said, 'Joey, get help. He's killing me. Joey, *please*.'"

Mama said, "Joey, that's enough."

"He *was* killing you, Mama. You know it."

O.W. met me at the passenger door. And we fought one another out under a blue sky between soy fields where lazy cropdusters dumped poison on summer soy. It was the sort of day when boys oblivious to their own deepening voices fished pond banks, sometimes forgetting the sunfish lashed on makeshift stringers, so that when the line was retrieved a water moccasin writhed where fish should be, and the shock would be gut-level so they'd never forget to suspect duplicity in all things. Though the fight was quick, I managed a left hook that broke one of O.W.'s front teeth and split my knuckle. He got this *I didn't know you'd do that* look on his face, blood running down his lip.

"You woodpussy," he said, and knocked my breath out.

And for the rest of it, the whole time while he kicked my ass, patches of blue sky shone through the cracks where wrist-thick snakes writhed on summer lines, I remember thinking *woodpussy?* What the fuck was *woodpussy?*

The big gray was the first whale me or Jimmy'd ever seen, coated in a slick layer of cottage cheese looking shit. It just lay there. No posters of living whales or Shamu with a beach ball on his nose or instruction on how to behave in such a beast's presence. Just a big, fat dead whale in a stinking trailer, getting hauled through towns like Lonoke, a skinny boy standing on the wooden platform below the monster sign. Leviathan's arrival was an annual deal. Somehow it'd got out that the thing could commune with the spirit world, so everybody and their mama came to stand in line. I hail from a people who're hell-bent on getting the last word, even if it means they have to speak it into a dead whale's ear.

Jimmy pointed at my duct-taped knuckle. "That needs peroxide. So is it true or a l-l-lie."

"What?"

"You know."

"It happened. You weren't born yet, but you were close."

"Bu-bullshit," my brother spat. "You didn't dream it?"

"She laid his cheek open with her fingernail. You know that scar."

"Shit," Jimmy said. "Why are we here?"

"These idiots believe it talks to dead people."

A lady up ahead of us lay down talking to the whale's head. She'd got down on her hands and knees, put her mouth up close to one of the filmy eyes. "Daddy?" she was saying. "Can you hear me? *Daddy?* Are you listening?"

"Shit," Jimmy said. "Who'd p-pay for that?"

I said, "Us."

The woman on her hands and knees was crying—the grief was hard on her, you could tell. I wondered what I'd have to say to the whale's head when my time came. I was thinking about the other-worldly feel of getting your ass kicked, how Mama's face looked upside down in the car—how on a railroad track she'd once hummed a tune from *Moon Over Naples*. Blue Traceleen in her church dress. And I was thinking how it was to have a brother, to see him grow up to be number 86, right defensive end for the State Championship Jackrabbits of 1985, to watch him throw forearm shivers and sing in the church choir on Sunday, then walk out the big double doors they'd so soon carry his casket through, six-feet tall and sawdust bronze—that was Jimmy. I loved every last thing about him.

Outside, somebody racked off muffler glass-packs—O.W.'s Chevy, it sounded like.

The woman cut us a hard look—she glared straight through us. Then she turned back to the whale, put her lips to the fetid face and kissed. "I know. I know you didn't mean to, Daddy. I forgive you."

It was embarrassing, the whale's big eyes like greasy saucers.

"That lady's b-bonko," Jimmy said. "Calling that stinking thing Daddy."

13.

I shower in the Super 8 bathroom, a little hungover, then head across the parking lot for coffee in the hotel lobby. The pool is peaceful. Eastward, a rusty sun rises over woods of leafed hickory and pin oak. West is delta land—cropdusters sputtering over soy fields and milo growing right up to the front porch boards of people whose mothers and fathers and brothers and sisters are buried right out in the backyard under chimney bricks. South is town itself, a strip mall rebuilt around the Willy Ray City Center after the killer tornado that blew the top off the P.O. and Lonoke Bank & Trust. Northward, the funeral home where Jimmy once lay, and now Mama. Across the parking lot, the Burger King drive-thru's jam-packed with bricklayers and concrete finishers come for sausage biscuits and coffee. Hillbilly music leaks out their windows, drinking songs about fucked up life and love. A long-hair in a Ford smiles when his food sack comes. He parks, lets her idle while he eats. He could be me, ripping open the salt and pepper packets with his teeth, dusting a gold hashbrown patty. He chews with his eyes shut, then puts her back in gear, drives on out to the job site where he'll bust his ass for the rest of his life, where his son's sons will bend rebar into monolithic footings, and one day a thousand blackbirds will fall from the sky and no one will know why.

The hotel foyer's empty and the coffee, as ever, is watered down, the doughnuts stale and the luxurious aromas from yesterday are missing this morning. Each breath is salty—like I've stolen and drunk a bucketful of the ocean where blues run amongst swimming turtles. Early, it's Arkansas-hot already, the wavy air rising up and hovering just above the Super 8's asphalt, clear over to the Knight's parking lot.

"Good morning," the voice behind my back says. It's the hostess's husband, razor creases ironed into the arms of his white shirt.

"Morning."

"Hot today."

"Yeah. Hot, hot."

"Do you find what you need?"

"Yes, sir. Mostly."

I stir two-percent into the watery coffee.

The man's nut-brown hand reaches into the refrigerator that was empty a moment ago. Only now there's a bowlful of oranges; one of these appears in his right hand.

"The blood oranges must not be missed. Take two if you like."

I accept the offering, take two oranges, step through the double glass doors.

In the AWOL Pathfinder, Renee combs Lara's long brown hair—one, two, three. She's looking at me, combing out the long tangles. "Dog, cat, mouse," Lara says, the mantra she recites when the teeth catch a knot.

"Will O.W. have food? Lara's hungry."

When Jimmy died, the house filled with fried chickens and hams, sweet potatoes, baked beans and banana pudding and doughnuts, Danish rolls and pork cooked three ways: *death food*, I remember. "There'll be food. A shit load," I say. She's got the radio on KHOG—the blues already.

"Ready?" Renee says. "I mean. Are you ready?" She's got this Rockerson way of looking at you, sweet as pie. "This doesn't seem real yet." She shakes her head side to side and I remember the first moment I saw her, framed in my doorway— *are you him?* she'd said, and it had all been unreal, how she'd appeared out of the blue in Fayetteville springtime when every last barbed wire fence was blown over with honeysuckle and the redbud had bloomed.

Lara's in my lap. She smells like the Peonie Princess shampoo Meg gave her in Florida a lifetime ago. My daughter's warm and tan. I say, "You ready to see Grampa, sweetie?"

She says, "Is MaMa's dog there?"

I say, "We'll see."

"Well I don't like 'we'll see' Daddy."

We begin the last of it—past Town Center, over the railroad tracks past

Main and Vine. We pass the new P.O. with its brick memorial commemorating the postal clerks who'd perished in the great tornado. Lonoke's one stoplight gets us just up from Simmon's Slaughter, where Deputy Biggs Self once felled a white Charolais bull with a .44 magnum. *Boom, boom*, the gun went, me and Trace driving back from Tastee Freeze with a sackful of double cheeseburgers.

Morning Glory climbs Bernice Holt's well-house trellis. When I was thirteen, I listened on our party-line telephone as Mrs. Holt told somebody named Werner that she wanted to put his thing in her mouth right that second. I heard it late one night while O.W. slept in his living room recliner. In front of him flashed an Indian's head in a red circle and the TV made this high-pitched sound like when the emergency broadcast system said *this is a test*. The station had signed off for the night. When I tiptoed into the living room to shut the noise off, O.W.'s eyes snapped open.

"What're you doing?"

"Turning it off."

"I'm watching."

Him and Mama never slept the same room.

"It's a Indian," I said.

Our house was entirely dark save the TV shine. O.W. looked at me through the gap in his outstretched black boots. Light was in his eyes. "Then I'll watch a goddamn Indian," he said.

I said, "Okay." And that's what he did; O.W. watched a goddamn Indian. By sunup, the screen had turned to snow, remnants of the Big Bang, I've since learned.

Years later, after Jimmy died, Renee and I'd meet him at a truckstop outside Greensboro, North Carolina, a stop on his IceLand route to Baltimore. We'd eaten dinner inside where men who smelled heavy of aftershave talked into phones connected up at each table, sipping coffee and smoking cigarettes. O.W.'d been best man in our wedding. Mama'd got herself into politics and was on a trip to Ocho Rios, he explained, somewhere in the Carribean. Her lupus was in remission.

O.W. looked me in the eyes, then Renee. "Do you think it's good for her? Ocho Rios?"

I said, "Beats hell out of Maybelline."

The waitress flirted with him, kept his cup full and offered him some more cherry pie. "I guess so."

"I'd go in a heartbeat," Renee said. "Right now."

O.W. swallowed coffee, and looked out the plate glass to the lot where empty trucks idled. "Mama needs to be careful," he said. Before we left, he led us out to the refrigerated trailer's padlocked double doors. He keyed the lock, stepped into the dark and out rushed a wave of frosty air. "Here," he said, lit up under a red trailer light. A whole gutted turkey hung dripping in either hand, big birds, twenty-pounders. "Happy Thanksgiving."

"*My god*," Renee said. "Can he do this?"

"Where are we going?" Lara asks, plain as day.

Renee's taking the back way in, the cut-through between Jackrabbit Stadium and Honeysuckle Drive, past the state policeman's house on the curve and the grown-over gully where I smoked my first joint.

I'm wondering, what was O.W. saying? People don't just die of their own accord. What was the story getting told about Mama? Heart attack in the hottub? Lonoke folk sniff every crook and cranny.

We make a left on Willy Ray, and way off I see our destination—the crooked mailbox shadowed by pines, the retarded neighbor boy Mama loved—now in his forties—mowing our grass, an offspring from an ancient pet rabbit still chained to a Silver Flyer.

14.

When you come to the home you've left behind, your old front door with the eight-penny nail driven into its face for the Christmas wreathe, do you ring the bell, knock, or just walk on across the threshold like you were never driven away? Say? Do you bustle your wife and daughter in front of you or step first to meet the other side head on? Is it best to turn and look at Jess Greyback's yard while the eye looks you over through the peep-hole, or press right up so the eye sees an eye? And how about this, the knock itself, what's the right way to do that—what code should be tapped on the door of the dead? Three slow, somber knocks? The staccato six? *knock-knock-knock-knock-knock-knock*? Is it inappropriate to use the musical seven-knock *duh-duh-duh- duh-duh, duh—duh* Beverly Hillbillies knock? Think about it. How long between knocks? And how many separate times do you knock before giving up? Is it proper to stand knocking at a door for, say, five minutes, while your daughter turns cartwheels in the nicely-mowed front yard and the forty-year old fourth grade neighbor's rabbits squeal in the heat and hump each other and shit through the chicken wire cages beyond the yard swing? Is it appropriate to ring the doorbell after first knocking and vice versa? Which comes first, knock or bell? If you own a cell phone, what is the rule on dialing the number of your drowned mother, telling the answering machine that you're standing at the front door this second, and how about goddamn opening up before you burn the frigging house down? Would that be pushing it too far? Is kicking down your mama's front door a feasible means of entry? Once O.W.'d caught me climbing through the kitchen window, dog-drunk, a bench warrant out for missing DWI court. Mama watched him hog-wrestle me down to the linoleum. She dialed Deputy Biggs Self, who handcuffed me and walked me out to the cop car.

"Get help, Joey." Mama said it like a line of theater.

"What do you see in that fat bastard?"

"Your father. And your brother's and sister's father."

If you smell chemicals from the hot tub mixed with the smell of your mother's hair, is it acceptable to scream *son of a bitch*? I mean, where do you find the rules of engagement for such a moment? Traceleen drives a powder-blue Camero up beside the Pathfinder. The windows are tinted. She gets out blue-faced as ever, cries when she sees my face. My sister holds her arms out.

"*Joey.*" Without the glasses her eyes are deep blue, like O.W.'s or Jimmy's. She makes her living taking care of insured people who are paralyzed, elderly or in some other general state of fuck-upedness. She takes care of people like Mama, only with money.

We hug. "Where's O.W.?"

"Daddy? I don't know." Trace looks at me and I understand that she's seeing Mama in me, and that's a jolt. Tears stream down her face. "Making arrangements, probably."

Lara's shy beside me. A red-headed hummingbird thrums by, hovers over Renee's head then hauls ass. "Christ," she says.

Trace is Mama and O.W. all mixed up, his big bones and body with her sweet face lines. We're sweating big real sweat. Trace holds a sackful of liter sodas—Pepsi, Mountain Dew. I take the sack from my sister. "What happened?"

On either hand, she's wearing the rings, wedding, engagement, anniversary.

"To Mama?" My sister's chin quivers. "Mama drowned."

"How?"

Trace's boy's name is Douglas. It dawns on me that he's inside the blue Camero, I can just see his outline through the tinted glass. He's big for his age, Mama's favorite, he reminded her of Jimmy.

A woman with TOOTS on her license plates drives up in a white Trans-Am with a big American flag sticker on the passenger door. She gets out in cutoffs, nods at Traceleen and sets a pie on our front porch. Dora Waymack's looking at us through the kitchen door window, I can feel her there. I smell the Hercules Plant spewing fifteen miles away in Jacksonville.

"Bitch," Trace says.

"Which one?"

Trace looks toward Dora's. "Both," she says.

"We've had a long haul, Trace."

"I bet."

"All I know's not too much."

"*Dougie*. Come out here."

The boy gets out, looks at his feet. We're all standing there in the drive where me and Jimmy used to wash our cars with buckets filled with suds from Mama's dishwash soap. From cages way across the yard on the neighbor's side, the rabbits stare pink-eyed at us.

"I keep feeling like Mama's with us right this second. Like she hasn't gone anywhere."

"Oh yes she has." Trace glares. "I threw up in the morgue."

Dougie sides up to Lara, wraps his arms around her and picks her clear off the ground.

"Daddy," she screams.

"Lara," Renee says.

Traceleen says, "*Goddamnit* Dougie."

Lara squeals, just throws her head back as if this is the happiest moment of her life, looks me in the face and says *Daddy*?—a good question—and we're all just standing there. I've mowed my way around this square of earth all those hot Sundays after meatloaf, watching the neighbor girl wash her yellow Pinto in cutoffs three houses up, the bikini straps loose on her white shoulders while the neighbor bathed his rabbits—cooing at them, saying things into their ears.

Next door, Dora stares. She's always called Mama at three a.m. to tell a joke or dish dirt or go on about how lonely it was to be a woman. She was a thorn in O.W.'s side. He called her a lesbian bitch, Mama said. *Dora, you lesbian bitch!*, he screamed out the window one morning at three a.m., her and Mama on the phone telling secrets.

Lara says, "Looky, *tunder*." Sure enough, a purple squall moves overhead, the leading edge of an Oklahoma cold front come out of the blue.

"Her casket's white," Trace says. "It's nice. Daddy left you a set of keys out on the electric box."

"Casket," Lara says. At my side under a tornado sky, my daughter says *casket*, she tries the word, the hard *k* ratcheting the roof of her mouth.

I'm home. Dead in the middle of Willy Ray, my own house with my own name on the mailbox. A post 9-11 *United We Stand* sign shines beside the plywood ramp where black skid marks prove Mama's driven her little power wheelchair out to the mailbox. Footprints scuff the tread marks. The box was knocked down once for one whole year—me off in Utah. On a summer trip, I watched Mama drive her wheelchair out, pick the box up off the ground, then drop it again when the mail was retrieved. The mail woman did the same. Harvell, my own name on the box. Dora came outside and applauded when I cemented in a new post.

"Can I see MaMa's doggie?"

Renee says, "Yeah, sweetie. If he's home."

"You ready, Joey?" Trace takes my hand.

Off to the driveway's left, ruts from Jimmy's gold Grand Prix.

I say, "Yeah," and we make the walk. *United We Stand*, the yard sign says. Cool air seeps through the frame, and on this leak I taste what's happened; the scent of terror and chlorine and flesh and blood misted over with Mama's own flowery room freshener named *Autumn Wood* or *Symphonic Bouquet, Potpourri aux Springtime—Eternally Yours*.

Behind us, Willy Ray Street has two ends, east and west—the entirety of the place once an orchard so remnant fruit trees gnarl every yard. Miss Caroline Tippet's pear limbs are strung with King snakes—gleaming six-footers—to bring rain, or impotence to some cheating man, whatever the old witch wants on any given day. Over there sits Mr. and Mrs. Penny Way Goff's run down shed, where the touched son—about my age and stuck for all time as a fourth grader with an affection for cottontail rabbits—has built chicken wire cages. When Mama was off in Jamaica with Shawn Terrence Lord, I watched O.W. get out of bed on a hot-hot night, walk out to the cages under a starry sky and just stand there, long arms at his side. It was real hot—the air-conditioner was out and O.W. walked outside. I already lay under the pecan. Mama was off drinking coconut drinks on the beach with Lord, though we didn't know that then.

Through the barbed wire, across the lime field, was the red barn where the head dance instructor from Milly's House of Tap sometimes met me, draped in a horse blanket, her skin white and warm. In heat like that, the Goff boy's cottontails squealed, a sound like wind whistling a hole. As far as O.W. knew, he was alone in the universe, under the night sky, Mama off with her lover, though he maybe didn't know that. Or maybe he did. O.W. reached in and took the white buck by its hind paws. Anything could happen on Willy Ray Street where the dance teacher—naked under her horse blanket—was to meet me in the barn below the lime field. The white gate would creak open and the horse blanket would part, then slide down her long dancer's legs.

O.W. bent over, sat the bunny down on the sweet grass, and I watched him with my own eyes, bend over and stroke the thing's back, shew it away with a backhand, so the white shape glided across the yard past me, through the barbed wire fence and down into the limefield, past the barn toward Harlan Bottoms and the strawberry fields where the pickers lay sleeping under the stars.

The air's on. Trace lets the door shut. Behind us, that suck-sound that closing makes.

Lara says, "It's dark in here."

She's right—light's no good for lupus patients, so every last window in the house has been covered with aluminum foil, and that covered with pull-blinds.

"He's here." Trace says it, brings me home.

Mufflers rack off outside, *O.W.*

15.

O.W. arrives on the front edge of a squall, same bruised color and low-low pressure as the F-5 monster that twisted into Lonoke County in 1976. I walk outside. The air smells like sulfur, like struck matches. We stand on the mown grass— son, mother, father, daughter, sister. No tornado, but a shit load of wind—sloppy raindrops splatter the concrete drive. Lara and Renee move close, we're all together when O.W. kills his engine, his blue-blue eyes through the passenger window. He's driving a new truck, a white closed-bed Chevrolet. We see each other.

What am I looking for? Hard rain polka-dots O.W.'s golf shirt. His flattop's trimmed tight. He walks to me straight-away, wraps both big arms around my chest and we hug. Just stand there like a real father and son and hug. We have history.

"Son," he says, pulls me tight against his chest. "I love you."

Behind O.W.'s back, Dora's curtains flutter.

"O.W." Talcum powders his neck—I smell it, hear diesels idling all through my childhood, a drunk's tremor in our foundation. "That's a nice truck."

He lets go. We stand there looking each other in the face. "Mama picked the color," he says. He looks like Jimmy, it strikes me.

Traceleen joins. And it's the three of us on the cracked drive.

"What happened?"

"She had a heart attack in the hot tub."

"How?"

"I've got a strong stomach, Joey."

Trace sobs. Her face is a mess. They viewed her together at the morgue. My imagination betrays me. Renee's got Lara in her arms, their pale faces. Wind whips our hair. Of a sudden, lightning, then thunder like a sheet ripping high up. From the courthouse a tornado siren wails and folk up and down Willy Ray walk out in their front yards and join us. There's Dora, in a flowery dress. She wants to say something, I can feel it in my bones. Dora looks straight at me, shakes her head and makes a sad smile to the sky. Rain, she says.

"What does that mean?"

O.W. looks at the palm of his ring hand. "Mama's better off," he says.

All the stuff you've ever heard about tornadoes is mostly true—how a Tastee Freeze straw gets driven through an oak tree and all the house trailers out at Gunter's Paradise get skinned clean as oranges. A litter of puppies gets lifted off a purebred mother and laid at the tits of a mongrel. A man gets his brains smashed out on one side of a table during a checkers game, while his twin—right across from him—experiences unspeakable serenity. The sun shines on one side of the street while apocalypse is wreaked on the other—*the devil beating his wife*, Mama'd say. The glut and gurgle of it, freight trains skidding on steel rails in the midst of creepy silence. Fish rain down from the funnel, feed pond catfish wind the uplift vortex and understand their dear friend Crow.

In May, 1976, when Aerosmith's "Walk This Way" was playing out the T-tops of all the jet-black Camaros, Lowman's Hardware and Grocery got hit, as did Templeton's IGA and Fred Woodhead's Feed & Seed and the slaughter house on the railroad track, where all the white bulls got loose and Deputy Biggs Self chased them all down Main Street with the sirens blaring, fire belching from his silver-plated .45. Lonoke Bank & Trust took it right on the chin—a dozen or so locked themselves up in the vault that got squeezed tight, then simply disappeared upward, delivering titles and one-hundred-year-old mortgage assessments up into the funnel's mouth. *Oh God*—if there's a Jesus, I'm dead on sure he'd choose a tornado like the class five honeybabe that came to us that day in Spring, 1976, when I was fifteen and Coach had us running 220s out on the cinder track, staring the mother down, daring it to come. Nobody was about to back that son of a bitch down though, so Coach fired all the blanks off from his starter's pistol and told us to crawl under something. It was the week before Panter Relays. The pole vaulters lay down with one another in the pits, and the high jumper cocked his red face to the sky. All the hurdlers ceased to hurdle, the shot, discus and spear were laid down and the milers made a circle of themselves in the infield, praying the way distance men will.

All our chins yanked up to the hooked tail and twisted shoulders. *No!* somebody screamed. Our sprint relay ran a slow quarter mile, one behind the other—not sixteen inches between us—saying *stick*, so the runner in front would raise his arm behind his back, splay fingers and take the baton, and in turn say *stick*, we'd seen Larry Gunn from Wabbaseka do it with the grey hood up over his afro, about to run a 46 flat quarter. *Stick*, he said on the curve. *Stick*, we said as the curve bent straight. *Stick*, we said it for that one slow quarter around Jackrabbit Stadium while the pole vaulters lay down with one another and the high jumper said *Geronimo* and cleared six-eight. It came over the Visitor's Side bleachers, about to rip up the stretch of green lined Bermuda where I'd made an eighty-yard run one autumn night when the frosty air was sweet with Stickum Coach had sprayed on my hands, about to destroy, even, the fifty yard line where I'd once made out with my girlfriend's big sister, one night after passing out at Grandma Dee's hospital room and waking up with this girl's sweet-smelling breasts in my face. *Please Jesus—if you're who you say you are, come home as the tornado that shines full of fish when the devil beats his wife.* Shine like the golden faces of shocked cheerleaders in the drainage ditch where we took refuge. Their red-pleated skirts flew up over their heads and one would scream out in prayer, "Oh Jesus, I'll use my mouth again, please," and another'd cried out, "I will never ever with Bill Lingo's daddy," and another, "Oh Lord, he'll not be tasting me again," and the one boy cheerleader goat-eyed and pink-faced, he bit back his confession. All these voices twisting. Sheets of roof tin spun over our heads, flashing light then dark then light. Around me, upturned faces in angel-light, girls whose skirts had flown up over their heads, who'd confessed the almighty sins of this carnal world, a harmony I too joined on my knees. I prayed my prayer. A gum wrapper slapped my face with the full force of a man's fist. I prayed harder.

The tornado was slow and deliberate and *real*, the sunshine coming through its thick shoulders where all relations of matter were made one. On my knees I stared into it, the glittering fish and tin and Lonoke County dust. I loved it with my heart's heart. She crossed Highway 89 and moved over the Junior High

School and the Middle, over the wood desk where my brother's blond head was cradled, toward the slaughter house where the white bulls would run amuck, so Mama'd see one get head-shot by Deputy Self. Right in our front yard, the fairy blood pooled. O.W. was hammer down through Kentucky at the time, thirty thousand pounds of slaughter turkey in tow.

And then the wind stilled and the girls' skirts righted themselves, which I was sorry to see, especially with regard to Fonda Whitehurst, whose purple panties seemed ripeful of the storm itself, whose confession has always held for me the most heft. "Little girl, daughter," she said. "Forgive me for what I've done. I'll comfort you. Where you are, sweetie, I'll come home to you. Mama loves you," she said, and I knew she meant it. And it was then, right as *love* rolled off Fonda's lips, that the great tornado of 1976 chose to let us be. The sun shone and red-headed hummingbirds began to dive-bomb us from the Visitor's bleachers. A ways toward town, the twister gleamed and we got up off our hands and knees. We grinned at each other and turned red. I put my arm around Fonda Whitehurst's pale shoulders; she was my sister now. Off in the distance, the bank exploded. People died that second. *Dear God*, Fonda said with this holy white light on her face, shining through the coils of her black hair.

Sirens sang out in the eerie light. Newly bound, we stepped into the deformed world.

Dora says, *RAIN*.

"Let's get inside." O.W.'s walking up Mama's plywood ramp, so its gut sags.

The seam I heard in his voice three nights ago, it's here. When his father died, I heard it then; same with Jimmy, that crack his voice showed through.

16.

Our customary seats: O.W. in the recliner, me and my wife and daughter on the love seat to his right, Traceleen over to his left, on the couch where Mama'd be, half-looped and moaning on pain killers. The chemicals I'd sensed through the locked door are fully realized now. Tough Man, Mama's little black and white Shih Tzu trots out through the laundry door, dragging a purple-striped tube sock—Jimmy's from football sixteen years ago. The dog trots pretty as you please, right up to Lara and leaps into her lap which flat out amazes my daughter—the most amazing thing. The TV's on—Bob Barker ogling big breasted contestant number three, *come on down, the price is right.* I feel outright sick. She'd scalded, I remember Trace saying. He's tried to cover the smell with Mama's potpourri.

The doorbell rings. When Traceleen opens, there stands Uncle Bold and Aunt Judy. "Good morning, Jimmy," Uncle Bold says.

O.W. glares.

"*Joey,*" I say.

"Sorry, Joey." He says, "Two crows," sips from a sealed coffee mug. Bold's a whiskey drinker, full of jokes and lies like the time his co-worker at Chesapeake Electric got sideways on a light pole, into the hot wire, so this man's shoes got blown a hundred feet into the sky and came flittering down like two crows. Two crows—Bold says to cheers a drink.

Tough Man yaps at Uncle Bold from Lara's lap.

"He's in shock," O.W. says.

"Is he?" I ask.

Renee goes to the bathroom down the hall, passing each of our senior high school photographs, the jumbo versions that Mama has hung one beside the other, me looking like who I used to be. Jimmy's the same, sweet and true, but Trace's changed most dramatically, still a shade of blue beneath the rouge.

"Grampa? Is he MaMa's doggy?"

Aunt Judy guides Bold to the couch. Evidence of my mother is everywhere to see, though O.W.'s clearly run the vacuum, and tried to dust, maybe. My stomach turns again when I picture what Renee's likely to find in the bathroom, anything at all's possible, they've lived ramshackle, Mama and O.W.

"How you been, Joey?"

"Fine, Bold. Real good. You?"

"I had a heart attack."

"You?"

"Yeah. Triple bypass. Nice hotel. That dark woman's a looker."

Renee floats back up the dark hallway. We nod.

Some guy's having a go at the price tag for a roomful—jet skis and a snorkeling set, fishing gear and a marine cooler, a fold up dome tent and a boatload of water accessories presided over by a redheaded model with bony hips. O.W.'s transfixed. The recliner squeaks when he moves. Light filters through the bay window drapes.

"We need to write the obit, Joey." Dougie's wearing a football helmet. He sits in Trace's lap, big as a bear.

The game show contestant guesses three grand, good maybe, because the redhead's beside herself, on the verge of ecstasy.

Trace beckons me to the kitchen table. It's covered with bills and newspapers and plates of forgotten food. A letter from Shawn Terrence Lord is pressed under a soup bowl where a couple of carrot wedges have hardened—no return address. *The Price is Right* ends with a bang—all the long-legged brunettes and blondes and the pointy-hipped redhead hugging and smooching the winning contestant who's slipped the snorkel mask over his face so his every word sounds like *snorka, snorka, gomp, gomp*. He pretends to breaststroke. Commercials come on. Bold and Judy chew doughnuts. Renee gives me her look from the loveseat—here we are, three million miles from her father's 70th, good old Cap with his pool and vodka tonics and the blue-green ocean. We've come a long way, a blur.

Trace shows me bits and pieces of my mother's lifetime: a marriage certificate, a picture of Mama with Hillary Clinton's arm around her, a bronze retirement plaque. "I want it to say something about the campaign."

"We got married in 1965. How long's that?"

Trace touches her chin to my shoulder. She's shaking. "We? I can't quit seeing. It's awful," she says.

I hug my sister, take her in, blood is blood. This moment: when trucks roll uphill, a rabbit rolls her pink eyes back for the squeal, all of us on the railroad track, we're on our knees, our mother's screaming *help*—the whale's breath in our faces.

"Where's her will?" I ask Traceleen.

From the recliner, his back to me, O.W. says, "She has none."

"That's not true."

The recliner squeals. "She show it to you?"

The briefcase—where I once glimpsed Shawn Terrence, Mama's goddamn prissy lover, that's where. I *know* and *know* and *know*—the picture my mind makes betrays me. O.W.'d have seen it by now, he would have looked there.

"She told me over the phone."

He studies me, his head twisted like an owl's, his muscled shoulder bones showing on either side of the recliner's back. Somebody's dusted off the big-framed photo of him and Mama, the one we'll use for her obituary.

Beside me, Trace has found the letter from Lord. She's reading the words.

"Mama was taking a lot of medicine." O.W. nods. "A boatload."

The air kicks on and the phone rings and spaceship-home winds dizzily. Outside, the storm's hauled ass and the sun's come out. Country boys from here to Batesville are kicking piles of cowshit amongst bitterweed and clover, harvesting belly-white mushrooms they'll boil into talk-to-Jesus tea. After a rain they grow straight out of shit into the light.

Trace says, "Daddy? It's the gravedigger. He wants to know where again." Lord's letter is in her hand, wide open.

"Where?" The word comes from his throat—gravel out a concrete chute. My father's out of the chair—moving fast. "I told him three goddamn times. Beside Jimmy."

I'll never know why, I say, "If he was a smart man, he wouldn't be a gravedigger."

Not three feet in front of me, the place on Mama's letter where Shawn Terrence says *Love, Me* in loopy blue cursive, O.W. looks me in the eye. "Dumb truck driver," he says. Then, to Trace, "In the goddamn ground. Tell him to dig a hole in the goddamn ground. Beside your brother."

Lara chases Tough Man through the laundry hall toward Jimmy's room, Mama's tomb.

"*No.*" I scream it too late.

17.

The hollow core door's locked inside out, an obstacle I long ago learned to jimmy with a half-hearted shoulder, only not today—every cell in my body says *no*. The laundry hall's dark, not a place to try to get your bearings. It reeks of overflow and powdered bleach and the smell that comes when a shit load of air freshener's sprayed to mask something really awful, so the hybrid is far meaner than the original. One Thanksgiving me and Mama'd laughed ourselves silly on this very spot. We'd just ironed and starched twenty some homemade dinner napkins, and I was teaching her how to French fold them into the *fleur de lis* we used at Buster's in Little Rock, where I waited tables. Mama'd got this idea we could use the napkins, set up honest to god place settings for a Thanksgiving meal. Fresh off the road, O.W. caught us at the tail end. IceLand had sent him home with this huge turkey and spiral sliced ham which he traded me for one of my napkins.

"Looky here," he said, "nice little hat." He sat the *fleur de lis* up on his burr flattop pretty as you please, so Mama started laughing and peed in her pants. Jimmy walked out his bedroom door and Trace joined in from the kitchen. We all got belly laughs and had a time. O.W. marched around singing "I'm Hen-ery the eighth I am! I'm Hen-ery Hen-ery the eighth I am, I am," the starched napkin blooming white and frilly on his head.

To my left, a door leads to the garage, stuffed full of plastic bags full of garbage and knick-knacks Mama was always collecting; I imagine the fake silk ribbons draped from the handlebars of a mini-bike that long ago leaked its oil onto the busted concrete—mother, father, son and brother, odd souvenirs from our family cemetery, along with untold wreathes and the hideous paintings of ducks and flowers and bird-faced boys. Mama's white Towncar is parked in there—the

one Renee'd borrowed while ours was in the shop. The power seats somehow got
screwed up, so my wife'd had to drive all over creation with her chest forced up
against the steering wheel, "so close the frigging horn honks," she'd said.

As ever, the bolt gives when I put my shoulder to it.

After Jimmy's wreck, I sat in here and read love letters from the girls who'd
call him beer-breathed in the middle of the night, talk him into a late drive like
the one that got him killed.

Out Jimmy's window, beyond the confines of this room, Dora—Mama's best
friend—is digging. I once witnessed her kill a rattlesnake with a shovel blade. Right
out in the backyard, she hung it with a garland of yellow ribbons from a tree limb.
In a dry year, snakes bloat from tree limbs all over the county. This second she's
wrestling a tree into a hole she's clearly just dug in her backyard. The sapling's
bottom-heavy. Dirty Dora snaps it this way and it dawns on me that she's planting
the tree immediately between me and her kitchen window, where I've often seen
her face shining behind the glass. It's a pine, a stout six-footer already, one day to
eclipse our whole house, the brown needles falling thirty feet into our backyard.
Dora's dogs want no part of her tree planting, both cockers hang back in the shade
of a bent-limbed pear. Our window hasn't been washed in a real long time; what
she's doing out there seems to happen in a gauzy far-off place. The heat's murder I
imagine—what in hell's she thinking. Dora, she's ever called Mama at three a.m.
to shoot the breeze, to dish the newest dirt about Brother Dell or Deacon Meloy,
whatever bucktoothed sixteen-year-old they'd been caught with now. How they've
both been spotted in a sedan sitting either side of a dark man sipping a whiskey.
O.W. calls her *goddamn witch* and worse. Like I said, he one time ran outside in the
middle night screaming, "Lesbian bitch, lesbian bitch." Anybody that stepped in
between O.W. and Mama was either a lesbian or a man about to get his face broken.
Dora and Mama'd talked right through 'til daylight when O.W. deadheaded off to
Tennessee. Not long after that, O.W.'d paid to have every last tree in our yard cut
down and hauled to the dump. Not even the pecans or apples were spared, one
great swath of harsh summer sun burned down on the once shady piece of street.

Now she's planting a tree. Dora can't see me see her, how she's got the tree
holed now, hammering a shovel over its tap root, spurting the whole thing down

with a water hose. A wand of white sage burns on the raw dirt of a manhole sized circle—what once covered the tree hole. Her lips move, witch prayer, maybe.

The tub thrums. The room's not really supposed to be a bedroom, more like a sewing room or a place to put laundry, more like a jail cell or an eighteen wheeler cab. Ten-by-ten, a hundred square feet, it's a small room with bad light. The sort of dimness you might find in the cellar of a house long ago covered by a lake, so the doors all waft open and shut to the home of eyeless things. Burnt flesh mixes with sweet gardenia—White Shoulders cologne—the scent Mama'd been wearing on her wedding day, when I stood between her and O.W. What's happened in here—inconceivable.

I stand in the room and it's hard to see. Outside is better. Dora lights a box match, puts fire to a cedar sprig, walks it clockwise around her pine tree. Life begins and ends: the big things in life, those moments when earth air sings, haven't they all come clothed in fire?

"Dumb truck driver," O.W.'d said out of nowhere. *Dumb truck driver?*

Fire's no friend of O.W.'s. He tried to light one in a cinder block house we lived in one time. This was a Saturday when I was ten, Jimmy four, maybe. Trace was not yet born. And it was this bright, cold Saturday, with loud glurps issuing from the barn where our one horse—a stumpsucker O.W.'d named Happy Boy—was sucking stall rails. For some reason I'd asked Mama if we'd all live to the year 2000, thirty years off in the future then. She got this crooked smile on her face, like Lara does, brown eyes twinkling.

"Why of course we will, honey. *Of course* we will." She looked off through the kitchen into the living room where O.W.'d carried in the lawnmower gas can and was giving the green wood a good dousing.

"Why, why in the world would you ask that?"

O.W. was straight sober. He tilted the gasoline can into the fireplace, soaking the wood. Then he carried it toward us and out through the kitchen door, came back in and took a box of kitchen matches out of the silver drawer. He went about his business—we could've talked about anything, me and Mama. Happy Boy grunted in the barn—we'd all live to 2000.

"Say Joey, why'd you ask that?"

O.W. struck the match. When it caught, a ball of orange fire whizzed over his shoulder toward us, past Mama's head, then out the kitchen door and back in again. The flame burst in the fireplace then came at us again. Two, three seconds maybe. O.W. stood and stared, like he could back fire down—that's what every fiber in his body seemed to scream—get out of my house, you don't belong in my house. He stared, *get out*, and for a while that's what the fire did—it disappeared, long enough to get its courage up. The three of us stood there looking into space, the burnt air between us, the way people do after a Pentecostal church service when somebody's handled a rattlesnake.

"*Lord, God*," Mama said.

I smelled singed hair.

"What on earth are you doing, Orvell?"

Out in the barn, the swaybacked horse said I love you and I imagined the rats in the feed room bin, how they go crazy when the light hits them, how they chew saddle leather. Life is truly miraculous, a real shocker—the way the fire walked over the trail of fumes, how it traversed the airy space. And O.W. standing there with his shoulders thrown back with that light in his eye. He'd brought gasoline into the house, lit the match; the fire'd singed the fine lashes off his eyes. Out in the garden east of our barn, stumpsucking Happy Boy'd walked out and was eating Mama's green tomatoes. He was singing "I'll Fly Away," remembering the green meadow days before his nuts were cut off.

"Of course we'll live, Joey," Mama'd said. "Don't ever be like him."

O.W., ox-strong cyclops of my dreams.

Maybe it's the noise behind my back that makes me turn, or the feel of being stared at by human eyes.

O.W. fills Jimmy's doorway. He levels his right arm, points the finger. "Don't that lesbo know she won't live long enough to see that thing grow?"

18.

The road O.W. drives to the funeral home is a rerun of my teen years. Farmboy, on the corner where the highways cross, where I used to ride Happy Boy and tie him to a bike post out front to buy bread the winter we burned our neighbor's Kentucky board fence for heat. Almost to the train tracks, Woodhead's Feed and Seed, next the slaughterhouse. Over there's Tastee Freeze and the new Willy Ray Courthouse Building with its jail where I'd bled the night Angel broke my nose and Mama'd had to post bail and hire one of the town ambulances to haul me to Saint Vincent's Emergency Room, where they performed the procedure that saved me from freakhood. First Baptist Church rears beyond the red light, only different now. The old sanctuary sits abandoned, emptied of the pew even where I'd once sat beside Mama and O.W. with my stomach growling and watched the stained light pass through Mother Mary and the white sheep and onto the thighs of the organist playing "Pow'r in the Blood." In some devilish competition with the Methodists and Pentecostals, Brother Dellwood Walker somehow swung enough tithes to build the new monster which covers an entire block and possesses no windows. What's a church without light? The new church looks deformed—a jutting bullfrog down Walnut Street this morning. We pass Sweet Dreams Flower World, the Church of Christ where no music's allowed—where they sing sweet a capella and the girls all have that perfect look on their faces, as if stationed somewhere between a Ninth Street whore and the patron saint of lost boys, where I had many, many fine looks up billowing skirts at the long, long legs of my girlfriend's one sister, whose black hair tumbled to her waistband, whose voice never cracked. On the right, Missy Clark's house where the mama and daddy didn't care for one second if she just up and lit a joint, passed it all around, the brother whacked out playing electric guitar with pothead Junior Barentine out in the garage, and about half the football team skipping two-a-days, smoking dope and bouncing up and down on the trampoline in Missy's backyard. Over there, a house Mama tried to rent once, but got turned down at the last second for bad credit, right as I was about to unload our stuff from Brother James Lonn Tupelo's truck bed. "No can do," an old fat man said, carrying one of those little Mexican dogs that look like rats with bitty pink hard-ons, a little pink collar hooked to a little pink leash. Somebody's garden—old Jack Lowman's?—is putting on a show, morning glory blooms violet against the green lawn.

O.W. is silent, though his CB.'s raising hell–*breaker, breaker,* it keeps saying. The storm's cleared, the air's fresh. The sun is out, mushrooms blooming in every pile of cow shit from here to Toadsuck Ferry.

"They're having a hard time." O.W. says it just when the funeral home's in sight, same place they took Jimmy. "She was scalded pretty bad."

A man who's now dead—kind of a mystic at U.A. who'd had a hair transplant, which maybe disqualified him as a yogi—once taught me a technique called *shape, volume, substance.* How you can picture a shape, say a bread bag, give it a volume, say half-a-gallon, then a substance, say pig shit; concentrate on your *shape, volume, substance* long enough and you can make any thought disappear. One of his students killed him, just walked into his office and fired a pistol into his head first week of school. So fuck *shape, volume, substance.* Vent air is chill in my face. In my mind, the phrase *strong stomach* makes conversation with *scalded* and *dumb truck driver.*

A monkey-bent man buffs a black limousine under the funeral home drive-through. O.W. kills his truck on the black asphalt painted with yellow lines. I know in my heart that my mother's dead. For some reason I think of Shawn Terrence Lord, Mama's lover from the campaign trail—I don't know why. O.W.'d shit, or maybe he knew—all that time on the road to puzzle through. This is where they brought Jimmy, where they rebuilt his face for the open casket funeral. Somebody stole the senior ring and Rolex off his big left hand. *Man,* what I'd give to go back before all that, be sixteen and head over to Missy Clark's and smoke sensimilla hooter and jump all day on the trampoline in her back yard, her big bouncy cheerleader titties going in semi-circles. Or just haul off and beat the shit out of the cocksuck who told Mama we couldn't move in, our stuff already at the front door, him going on with that nasty little rat dog with its pink dick laying on his arm.

The man polishing the limo is a dead-ringer for a chimpanzee, the curl in his back and the dark brown hair growing right up his shoulders and neck, polishing a car the deep purple of a crow's wing. I'm thinking about Shawn Terrence Lord—by no choice of my own. O.W.'s driven us here with the air on high, C.B. chattering and the midget TV playing *One Life to Live*. All those years ago, after the truck rolled uphill, he'd let me believe that he was a warlock, that gravity had no hold on him. I remember snow, the roadside hippies scared shitless when O.W. got down on his air horn. What else?—the Tilt-O-Whirl mirrors, antelope chewing sage under a turquoise sky, the freak chill on me.

"I don't want to see her, Daddy."

"That's fine."

Cigarette butts are strewn the entire length of the home's front stoop—just like last time and the time before. Mama's handwritten obituary is folded in my front pocket. I'm in shorts and river Tevas, the fingers on my right hand still cut up from twenty-pound test.

"Mama'd want me to say *I love you*."

O.W. breaks up again, just a little, his bottom lip quivering. "I want her to look pretty."

"I don't want to see her."

"I understand."

We're outside the front double doors, getting eyed by somebody on the other side. I can feel the eyes on me, evaluating the situation, choosing words.

"She's in a better place."

Many of the cigarette butts—and I mean there are hundreds smoked to degrees that vary between not at all to deep into the nub—are printed with lipstick, Maybelline, no doubt, probably stuffed on the same line where Mama worked.

"Better than where?"

Cars pass lazily out on the highway, beyond the hot parking lot. A decade plus some ago, we'd all driven up to this same parking lot, climbed out and looked at Jimmy laying on grey crushed velvet in his jet-silver casket. Mama'd passed out, knocked the corner of her head on a floor tile and made a sound nobody should ever hear.

"She was scalded real bad. I've got a strong stomach."

"How? I don't want to see."

"She had a heart attack." The door swings open behind our backs and out comes the sick-sweet air. "Mama drowned of a heart attack," O.W. says.

19.

In Salt Lake there's this Chinese restaurant we like—call it the Golden Dragon—that shares its eastern wall with a mortuary. The takeout's out of this world, and for a few dollars they'll deliver. For some years we opened our front door to steamy eggrolls and ham-fried rice, hot and sour soup and Admiral's Chicken, then Lara's pre-school route took me by the place right downtown off First South. The first sight sobered me—a horned golden dragon spilling across the plate glass. Inside, a man in glasses counted money out of a cash register. To his right, close enough to reach out and touch, the eastern wall where every morning the sun rose up over the eviscerated sewed-shut dead. All that karmic energy passing between, it was more than I could take. For one thing, what happens on the other side really is inconceivable. When I was a cub reporter for *The Lonoke Star*, the undertaker's wife crashed eighty-five miles an hour into the side of the Willy Ray Courthouse and got trapped inside with the Dale Carnegie Instructor of How To Win Friends and Influence People at Jackrabbit High. Firemen had to cut them out with an oxyacetylene torch. It was big news, eclipsing that year's arrival of *Leviathan* even, the undertaker's wife crushed behind a dashboard with her lover.

"She loved to smile," the undertaker said.

I scribbled that in my notebook, *loved to smile* I wrote. "How can you do this to your wife," my first ever question as a reporter. "Like this," the undertaker said. He made a few sutures inside her mouth. "I'm giving her the second smile this second."

"Second smile?"

The smell was how a cavity tastes. He showed me to the stainless steel gurney, inclined at an angle, where fluids are sucked up through razor spikes in the back, drained into this industrial vat with organs and whatnot. Teeth must be extracted sometimes, especially if the family has requested the face called *Happy with Jesus*.

"Yeah, second smile," the undertaker said and demonstrated how pieces of styrofoam were sewn into tiny slits in the gums, "the one for eternity." Then he wheeled her through a bolt-locked door into a room where refrigeration blew down upon us. "We call this the *fish room*," the undertaker said, as if confessing the key to the universe. I remember Jimmy in his casket, how I leaned in and touched his face, his hand, how the cold ran me through.

Now, standing just inside the double doors of the Lonoke Funeral Home, this heavy girl with green eye shadow says, "Gentlemen, I'm Cheryl." She says it so it comes out *Shurl*—not that there's anything wrong with that. "Welcome," she says.

O.W. says, "Thank you, Shurl," and shakes her hand three brisk times. She focuses on me, on the crick of my nose, gauging, I imagine, how many slithers of styro-paste it would take to put a smile on my face forever.

"You've got to be Joey."

"Yes."

"I'm not from Lonoke. But if I was, I'da known you."

Shurl takes my hand and gives me the look, the way a poker dealer says hello when you sit down to the game and it's time to make bets.

"Where is she?" O.W. asks.

The overhead lights have a tick, like something's sucking way too much juice. "Mrs. Harvell," Shurl says, "rests now in our Exquisite Farewell Room." Her little heels make no sound on the carpeted floor. "This a-way."

I say, "I don't want to see her."

Shurl's smile is inflected in her voice. "We understand," she says. They must give lessons for this at those national conferences in Las Vegas where mortuary people unite by the thousands for meetings about the big news on DNA certificates and the lowdown on how to do twins. "I'll be right back for you."

Here's what it's like—I'll try hard. Take acid, add maybe half a gram of cowpie mushrooms and a dozen black beauties on three cups of expresso after smoking a whole pack of clove cigarettes and eating hash brownies while smoking the rugby team's four-hitter bong loaded with skunk and watching Vertigo six times after midnight, throw in a gutted aligator gar singing "Eleanor Rigby" on the side of the road by the concrete sign at the county line that says PREPARE TO MEET GOD on one side and JESUS IS COMING SOON on the other, only somebody's painted I LOVE TO COME on the Jesus part, and add to this the semi-truck rolling uphill and all the dreams where undertakers wash their wives' hair and sew styrofoam into gum slits and maybe, maybe, *maybe* you can get close to seeing this shiny-toothed Shurl walk up the hall, the whole time looking me in the face and smiling the smile that knows the ins and outs of things.

"Here we are." Shurl's teeth are brilliant, though she's on the dumpy side, heavy in the hips and thick-wristed. Freckles show through her rouge. But she's spritely, I can tell that. She's the boss here, no way around it.

I follow her into the office, the walls all hung with degrees that undertakers get. Her desk is massive, a glass-covered phenomenon. Shurl sits in a big leather chair that makes her the tallest thing in the room. She spins it sideways to face me. There's nothing on her desk, it's a complete blank reflecting ceiling spray glitter.

"Your skin," she says. "You've been in the sun."

"How is she?"

"I have something for that burn. You have her skin." Shurl takes my measure. "A cream to erase the red out, I mean."

Funeral home air is not breathable—I nailed that first go round. "We've been at the beach."

"The beach," Shurl says. "I can doctor your burn."

"How's Mama?"

Shurl regards me. "Mrs. Harvell is *cosmetized*." Her face shines on the desktop—two Shurls, one the inverse of the other. "You got the obit?"

"It's handwritten."

"Aren't they all? No problem. Though some's neater than others."

The air's turned way down chill, so I feel my flesh and blood and breath—I'm all in my body. Life in the now, how the yoga people say it. I reach in my pocket, find my balls have entirely retreated. Across the glass tabletop, the glass reflects my mother's obituary, her résumé in reverse. Trace and I drafted the thing on Mama's own kitchen table, on top of bills and greeting cards, old newspapers and the slit open letter from California with Shawn Terrence Lord's rendition of *Josephine* looking girlish and odd.

Shurl reads and nods. "Looks all right. She'll be in tomorrow's *Democrat*. We got a picture already."

Her eyes light up through the glasses. A moment passes. She waits me out.

"Cheryl. Was my mother hurt?"

"*Hurt?*"

"Was there a report?"

"Report?"

"A death certificate."

Behind my back, the door swings inward, and a clean-shaven man walks very upright into the room. He's wearing a muted tie, gray with no design. "How are we this morning?"

"Two more," Shurl says. "Must be a scorcher out there."

He sees me and raises his brows. He's somehow related to the monkey man outside, I can tell that much. "This is my husband," Shurl says. "Mr. Harvell here has particular questions, Bruce. Can you help him?"

Shurl's husband cuts her a look. "I'm afraid not this second," he says. "Bless you."

Shurl says, "She's cosmetized. We did the best we could." She looks me straight in the eye. "You know it's been four days?"

"Is Mama okay?"

"Is she *okay*? Child?"

"Was she injured."

Shurl shakes her head. "Says here you been to college. Surely a college boy knows what happens to a human body after four days dead." Shurl looks me through, clicks her fingernails on the glass. "I'll call if I have questions. Your viewing's tomorrow at three."

She stands.

I say, "Thank you."

Shurl smiles the smile she's been taught to smile. "We're here for you," she says, holds out a hand. "Let me know what I can do you for."

Way off somebody's talking in a place I can't see. The words are barely audible.

20.

Outside, I drink the air and light. A horse neighs in the field across the highway and I begin to pick the cigarette butts up one by one and throw them in the sand-filled ashtray at the far end of the concrete stoop. So many cigarettes, each one a prayer? A healthy cedar—I can't remember this tree, was it here for Jimmy's viewing or has it grown since?—rises in the middle of the circle drive. As if here for me alone to see, a red-headed woodpecker hammers the hard trunk, maybe fifteen feet off the ground, a sound that marries my childhood to this moment. The woodpecker, what Grandpa Stepwell'd call *peckerwood*, which just as easily became *peckerhead* out of his mouth, is going to town, a jackhammer of blood and bone and feather up high in the hickory fork, sunlight full on its red head, surely making enough sustained noise to get through the funeral home walls, up into the deluxe caskets in the fish room, through even the false membranes of Mama's sealed shut ears in the Exquisite Farewell Room with O.W. I hope like goddamn hell so, that woodpecker music reachers the sleepers.

"Hep you?" The monkey man who's been polishing limos hops up on the stoop, a little whisk broom and dustpan in one hand.

"Help me?"

He's already bending, sweeps and dumps—in jean shorts and a tee shirt, blue Addidas running shoes, worn on the inside arch. I can't know that in two days he'll be the most darkly quiet chauffeur I'll ever think to remember. "Looky here," he says. "Cooter's cousin."

"What's that?"

He holds up an inch of joint, sniffs it. "Hooter," he says. "Cooter's first cousin. Meet Mister Hooter."

Before the words are dead, he's lit the roach, breathed out smoke and handed it to me between thumb and forefinger. "*Ear*," he says. And without thinking I take the smoke into my lungs, hold it there. The woodpecker's alarm is fine from the hickory, a good note, between the dead and the living, a little music for the here and now.

"Thank you."

"Thank yee," he says, green eyes like slag glass.

A white LTD drives up in the lot beside O.W.'s truck. Out gets an overweight woman in a flowery dress and her skinny husband whose name, I'll bet my soul, is Claude. Her man gives her free rein, she's boss—I've seen her a thousand times. She was my Sunday School teacher, my fourth grade music teacher, the woman whose arm was broken when the black tornado hit our post office in '76. She's the pianist at a church where people touch rattlesnakes. I bet money she calls herself *Claude's jewel*. Three reasons occur to me why they're walking up to the newly swept stoop, where the monkey man who'd lit up the hooter has just skittered away to the garage. The peckerwood screams and batters the hickory violently when she passes. Claude's jewel throws an evil look up into the tree, and her husband looks pitifully at his shoes. A heavenly smile spreads across her face the instant she sees me. Maybe, I'm thinking, this is Shurl's mother, come to give her some shit for putting my mind to work on a body four days dead, how it might be, how Mama might be.

They nod at me and smile like Christmas morning, walk on past, the door opens and shuts, more of the sick-sweet air, only spiced up with woodpecker racket, his hammering redoubled with the woman's feigned threat.

A concrete bench appears at the far end of the building, where I can see that the horse that neighed from the far pasture is a big paint. Mostly white, his colors bleed through. Carved on the concrete bench—*Love Wins All*. Inside, O.W. has seen what's inside Mama's casket. Love wins all? Something's turning here, a piece of my mind connects *dumb truck driver* with when semis roll uphill outside Rawlins, Wyoming. Snakes writhe on fishing lines, I see them where fish ought to be. The instant my knuckle cracked O.W.'s incisor, I heard *get help, he's killing me, Joey!* Love wins all? Shawn Terrence Lord stares from Mama's briefcase— hadn't she prepared to die? Didn't we have that talk? I'm sitting here, obliged to pay attention. This flat piece of delta land bleeds east to the Mississippi River, seventy miles from where I sit, the West Helena bridge where the blues man jumped off and swam with a spoonbill, and it's said that boys fishing the caved-in banks still find Spanish armor and rifle balls amidst the mounds where bone shards lay in long grass like wavy hair. *Love Wins All*, that's something Mama'd say, or maybe just *go love, Joe. Can't you just turn loose and love. Don't wait for fire or flood. Go Love.* The flame-headed woodpecker—for all time now a spirit bird sent to hammer its message into my hard, hard Stepwell head. Tilt-O-Whirls blind in the summer snow.

Dumb truck driver?

After Jimmy died, me and O.W. got close. Having a brother made me part of him, in Jimmy our blood mixed—he was our bridge. Jimmy was drinking beer when he missed the dark turn out on 319. Traceleen's prom was the night after; in the picture, the fake light glows on her face. The photographer's shadow—an arm? a shoulder?—darkens to an edge. My mother and my father behind there somewhere, stricken. We were a family, a fucked up one, but a family.

What would Jimmy make of this, Mama drowning in a hot tub in his bedroom?

Was his ghost witness?

His clothes still hang in the closet and the plaque from governor's school is crooked on the wall. Mama'd been sick a long time, real sick, heartbreak sick since the car wreck. With the exception of the Clinton campaigns and the Ocho Rios thing, she'd been hurt to the bone with systemic lupus. Her body devoured itself. She'd prepared to meet God, made arrangements, asked me to deliver the eulogy. Then she lived. Jimmy'd been spared the midnight phone call with O.W.'s voice straining on the other end. He'd never had to hear that his mother was dead, that she'd had a heart attack that no coroner would ever corroborate, that she'd been scalded half-a-day in 104 degree water, that there'd be no lakeside cabin vacation, that Mama'd cut O.W. off from her insurance settlement—just up and taken his name off the account after he'd spent a quarter of the money on four wheelers and false teeth. Jimmy'd never attend a viewing and he'd *never, never, ever* hear Shurl talk about what happens to a human body after four days dead. He'd never puzzle the word *cosmetized* and he'd never smoke dope with a man resembling a howler monkey outside a cigarette butt strewn funeral home. He wouldn't know that they could make you smile forever. He'd never confuse a wedding with a funeral, and he'd never get Cain and Abled by Brother Dell or drive inside the

Stepwell cemetery and sleep there on his own spot, cows mooing off beyond the ponds and fences and forests of Solgahatchia on the Trail of Tears.

He'd never ride in a funeral party, one that rattles down muscadine-lined gravel roads in Arkansas, past hunt clubs and fall-down homesteads. He'd never piss his name on the patch of earth that would someday have him, do the Stepwell jig across bitterweed and Brown-eyed Susan on the hill that forever overlooks a lightning-struck tree where cows go on chewing the green green grass of home. He'd never be appointed his brother's keeper or lay block around his dead, the trowel's metallic shring singing out through the hickories. He'd never learn the old finisher's trick of brushing seam cracks with a fine paint brush, conjoining the granite to stone. My own maternal grandfather showed me the trick in a thunderstorm when he, very well-bourboned, danced until he fell down on his own spot, then mine, knocking pipe fire out on his prosthetic leg. The straight lines and stone grit between us, the physical work of all this, what Dirky Lee will never get in a million years, watching my mother's father lay down the heavy stones around his own father, who, in turn, had once lain down the big stones for his own father—the sons of four generations of Stepwells buried at the blocked-in feet of their fathers.

Once, stars glittering on the stones, I unfurled my sleeping bag beside my brother and told him I wished it was me. I'll trade, I said. This was August, around the first birthday he missed. How I puked up the sky. The night sang out with bull frog and cicada and whippoorwill, those three hard notes sung again and again forever. And the moon shone on his stone where it said:

Here Lies Our Precious Son
James Steven Harvell
August 25, 1966-May 9, 1986
Romans 8:38-39

I mixed my own blood in the mortar, the seams between the stones I laid for him, the footing, the stork-white gravel raked over his chest. The metallic shring between me and the stone world. Here with my mother's people. My bed made for the night. The good sleep that follows the good work, the dreamless sleep.

Jimmy'd never have to ask his father if he'd killed his mother.

21.

O.W. sits down beside me, he joins me on the *Love Wins All* bench. All is quiet. And it's one hot mother, I mean it, people just don't know how weak-kneed Arkansas can make you in the summer time, when the snake doctors ride each other across the bermuda grass and a lawn sprinkler reminds me of Mama's one-legged daddy, how he'd hop through one set up in his tomato garden, squealing *who-ee! who-ee!* after hulling purple hulls. O.W.'s father was a driver just like him, had in fact got him started at Texarkana Motor Freight straight out of high school. I remember the old man's decrepit Cadillacs and whiskey breath, how he'd put me on his lap and work the accelerator with his feet and let me drive the back roads outside Little Rock. And once, on the bright August morning while Mama birthed Jimmy, I picked six or seven bloody red tulips out of his front yard—a gift for Mama and my new brother. He lay me across a bed and whipped my ass with the buckle end of his belt for a good long time. Mama hit the fan—"he beat my son for picking damn flowers?" she screamed at O.W. while Jimmy squalled in the basinet she'd made from her wedding dress lace. "Eight Royal Burgundies," O.W. told her. "He'd a shot me." And ever after, the tulip was a sign between us. Out of the blue, one would show up with a note saying, "Thank you, Joey—I'll never forget," or some such. She never forgave O.W.'s old man that one thing—whipping my butt for picking tulips, not even on the day of his funeral, when O.W. wept over the old man's casket.

"She's pretty," he says. "A little heavy on the make-up, but pretty."

The white horse nickers and the sound of cars on the highway fades in. I'm entirely here, on the *Love Wins All* bench with my father. I was best man in his wedding. I'm adopted. He's quiet for a second, the hickory swishing a little in the hot breeze. It's a moment we've come to in life, no hiding from this. I fear him.

I love him, the way he danced a silly jig with the *fleur de lis* on his head so we all laughed till we cried. My father.

"*Pretty?*"

Traceleen's Camaro revs into the lot.

"We'll go ahead with the viewing," O.W. says.

She's walking toward us, my sister. She walks across the lot and sees us, blue daylight on her face. The words *pretty* and *viewing* twist.

Trace's car shimmers. *Pretty?* I've always wanted a Camaro, the kind Kelvin Knight used to drive with his feet while sitting atop his T-tops, blaring Aerosmith, jumping the railroad track, cutting the Tastee-Freeze loop. That's Lonoke—people want Camaros, the throaty pipes and windows that leak dope smoke and incense and graveyard makeouts. Car wrecks on prom night, moans behind bucket seats. That's where I'm coming from, Lonoke goddamn Arkansas, where your Mama ends up tended by somebody named Shurl and people go around burning at the heart root for a Camaro, pray to Jesus, God and the Holy Ghost for the jet black Z-28 with swivel seats, a cassette player and Jensen coaxal speakers. Lord God in heaven, goose it, sound the double glass packed pipes, roll me with the silver rims. Take my eternal soul for a T-top. Bury me in a swivelled bucket seat.

Pretty.

We go into conniptions for the Trans Am version like the one loaned to me by the mother of the girl I played guitar for in the Miss Jackrabbit Pageant. She couldn't sing a lick, and it was real embarrassing down on the basketball floor under the flood light with eyes on us from the Visitors and Home side, her ripping "You Light Up My Life" to shreds while I finger picked the melody on a round-backed Ovation. *Man*, she sang bad, but her mother let me have her Trans Am for a weekend and I drove the Jesus out of the car, really, raced it down Highway 38, a hundred and twenty, a hundred and thirty. I cruised Little Rock, got happy and somehow picked up Sweet Sweet Connie from that "American Band" song and we had a fast ride after Beat The Clock happy hour at Cajuns.

"*Pretty?*"

He nods. I can smell it on him, her. The truth. He's seen. He's seen my mama. This second, he sees me see it in his eyes.

The air is still, all quiet like church. A held breath, a vacuum.

I say, "Tell me the truth, Daddy."

The fire-headed woodpecker flies, its silver wings bent.

My father looks me in the face—I see my brother in his eyes, the morning we all stood for the photograph with the dead deer head, how shell-shocked he was when Brother Dell cast the first dirt into Jimmy's grave hole and everyone sang "Amazing Grace" under the hickories.

Trace is on us. "Well?" She accentuates her skin's natural blueness with powder blue eyeshadow. She refused to see Jimmy after. My sister offers a hand to each of us. Mama's rings, I see again, shine on five fingers. This is the world now.

O.W. says, "Mama looks pretty."

22.

Before the six o'clock viewing, Renee, Lara and I join Uncle Bold and Aunt Judy for happy hour in their hotel room, which happens to be a unit me and Renee stayed in once, home for Christmas. We've made love on the sleeper sofa, sloshed jug wine into the heat and air unit. The afternoon's peaceful, a few kiddos splashing a beach ball around the pool, a trucker reunited with his family under the treated lumber gazebo, us in the northern wing, close enough to the Burger King to hear drive through orders. "*Ever-thing,*" somebody's saying. "*Everything?*" says the loud speaker. A raised voice says "*Ever-thing,*" plain as day. The loud speaker blurts, "*Everything?*" We all hear: "*Won't you please just give me ever-damn thing. Hear? Ever damn thing.*"

Bold laughs out loud. "*Everything,*" he says.

Renee snorts. "That's funny," she says, tears in her eyes.

People from the outside believe us Arkies marry our sisters and spend all day shooting hogs indiscreminantly off fall-down front porches where retarded banjo players fish for chickens. The truth is worse, probably. He's chainsmoking, Bold, going off about this eastern shore restaurant called Gunny's where the onion rings are big as bucket lids.

"I mean it, Jimmy" Bold points the lit end of a cigarette at me. "Bucket lids."

Judy's in a teri robe with her black hair coiling down, consoling Renee while Lara plays dress up with things from the dresser drawers. She drapes a lacy bra across her chest, sashays into a gauzy blouse. The TV's on the weather channel, these bunny-eyed women in low cut blouses forecasting heat followed by low pressure, then more heat. "*Hot, hot* and more *hot*, coming at you," the raven haired one says. I'm verging between Bold and the weather women, onion rings you can stick your fist through, and the heave-hoe of breasts between shots of storm maps dopplered across tornado alley.

"I guess you've been on high alert," Bold says. He swigs vodka tonic. "It's a hell of a thing." A funnel cloud's been spotted south of Tulsa. Warnings now stretch from Fort Smith through Pope County. The twister sighting has the blonde forecaster's blood up—you can see it in her cheeks.

Lara clacks Judy's heels over the bathroom tiles. Renee looks me through— how long does it take to fall out of love? Our Lara holds us together, her and my genuine affection for her people

Before Lara was born, Cap told us the story of how he got stuck in an Esso parking lot with a Gremlin-full of Stinger Missiles, one of which somehow ignited in the trunk, so when he opened up to check, it got loose down on the concrete, spun circles and made a general spectacle of itself, though it never actually blew up. No one knew, not even Meg. Not until they came out for Lara's birth, and ended up waiting a whole month in snowy Salt Lake. They stayed from December clear into January while Renee went toxemic and just kept on not going into labor, her feet swollen thick as sidewalk bricks. The night before they finally gave up and flew on back to Florida, high on Vodka tonics, Cap started telling the story and didn't stop. It was snowing outside, the plows making little sparks on the road as they went in the dark. Cap talked and talked, not looking at any one of us, cradling his drink and filling it when it was empty. He told all this and more, so that I loved him genuinely and said so several times over, because I was only maybe a knock or so behind him on the vodkas. The next morning, they'd be gone. Three days later, Renee went into labor, a forty-hour ordeal which she tried without painkillers. Lara would be born at 2:53 a.m., and I'd hold her to my chest, say, "She looks like my mama," and feel haunted.

After Cap finished, after he'd told all about the Gremlin and the missiles in the Esso parking lot, we all stood up and hugged and wept. The Christmas lights were still up, a few of the bulbs blinking. We all walked outside together—me, Renee, Cap and Meg. The snow fell in our hair. Renee hugged her mother and so did I. Before she let go, Meg squeezed my arm, then let me help her into the passenger seat. Cap said, "I love you two," and walked to the door of the car and got in. It was cold—fifteen or so. Renee should've gone back inside. We all had colds. But we stood there waiting for them to leave, after a month in the Scenic Inn up the street, waiting out the holidays for their first grandchild. Presently, the door opened. Cap got out and walked carefully on the slick street. The taillights caught him in the face just as he embraced his daughter. He was a man who hurt—I could tell that. Way deep down, this man hurt. And they hugged each other in the snow for what seemed like a long time. Then Meg beeped the horn. The car slid a little on the street and they were gone.

"What do you mean? High alert?"

Outside, under the drive-through check-in, a man I know, but can't put my finger on, steps out of a white rental. A red-headed hummingbird taps the window glass, thrumming the air. When our dog, Moon, died, I wrapped her in owl's wings clipped from a roadkill bird somewhere in Illinois, a road trip home for a sudden heart stint Mama got dragged into. We layered the bottom of the hole with broadleaf sage and dog biscuits, her food bowl and water. She was sixteen, a hundred or more in dog years, the remnants of North Carolina—our trial child. A chunk of life, a pet like Moon; when we mourn, we mourn for ourselves. I know the man in the dark pullover, like a light left on in a room across the street I once visited, only the furniture's rearranged and a rubber tree grows where the unfinished duck painting once leaned. The man from the moon, he's come.

Judy sits beside me, floral smelling, honeysuckle. "Your mama," she says. "Sick like that so long?"

When we stayed in this room before, Mama left a note outside on the windshield. *Dinner's at 7:30, Sweeties*, it said. Three boys, brothers, rip up the pool. And the man walks to his room, the easternmost wing, whoever he is.

"She was getting better. We planned a vacation on the lake."

Judy sips jug wine from a plastic motel cup. She's lost her own mother, O.W.'s, who maybe overdosed or something, I've never been sure. Judy looks at the floor. "It's a hard thing."

"How?"

We meet eyes. "Waiting to die," she says.

"Mama didn't want to die."

The hummingbird hovers outside the picture window, its beak just skimming glass. "O.W.'s been on pins and needles."

"We had a cabin on Greer's Ferry. We were all going to Blue Clouds."

Judy swipes tears. "It's a strange life," she says.

Lara leaps up beside me in a tee shirt with two crabs arm wrestling. Renee sits beside her, all these times I've dragged her to Arkansas, to Grampa's lake trailer or the family cemetery—blackberry picking in the Solgahatchie bottom. The liquor sears my throat, only for a second.

"Daddy, I saw a hummingbird."

"Me, too," Renee says.

"Out there," my daughter points.

At the drive through, a high voice asks for a Whopper. "Double Whopper," it says.

"So Daddy's been on pins and needles?"

Bold says, "We all have."

"Well I haven't."

Bold nods.

"Mama was getting better. She was herself again."

"That's the worst part," Judy tells me. "I'm so sorry."

And we all drink until it's time, the three boys raising holy hell poolside until the dark hostess calms them with a single look through the chain link gate. Afternoon in Lonoke, not far from catfish ponds stocked with blue channel cat where witchdoctors ride each other and wrist-thick cottonmouth sun on levee banks. Peaceful evening, the heat breaks some and all the penned catahoolas out at Gunter's Paradise sleep deep and dream of the instant when rain stops and the Man sets them free for chase, the good scent of coon on washed air. A sit-down fish fry begins at Willy Ray park where little leaguers drip snow cones on their mama's lawn chairs. Somebody prays *Lord Jesus, forgive our sin.* Miss Jackrabbit stretches both tanned arms above her head baring four fingers of belly flesh. Eyes meet. All these souls waiting for what happens next. Maybe *Leviathan* will arrive, or mule-faced woman or somebody'll have one hell of a carwreck or hook a ten pound bass, anything at all is possible in Arkansas on viewing day. Drowned of a heart attack nigh unto summer solstice: dumb truck driver. *Solstice*: sun stand still. Father-sun, the bridegroom cometh, he breathes the Holy Ghost fire.

23.

Her picture's propped up on an easel beside the casket where O.W. greets guests. Inside the wooden frame, Mama radiates. She'd get up this second and try to make us feel better. Say she's so sorry and give us all bear hugs, tell us to cheer up, keep on the sunny side, love wins all. Mama'd forgive us all our wrongs. She'd be dressed in red with her black hair shining on her shoulders, brown-eyed, that wide, real Stepwell grin that nobody can fake, about five seconds from tears of joy or sorrow or rage or laughter. Mama'd know how to run this show. Right now was the moment she'd planned for: the *Last Will & Testament* reading, because she goddamn wrote one about a hundred times, only my people aren't legally minded, so no lawyer ever signed off on the fucker. On good cotton rag, she wrote *go love* and *rejoice* and *dance all night*. She'd mean it to puncture our grief, leaven this moment with laughter. Mama'd start with a joke, a salty one about Baptist preachers and bucky-toothed cheerleaders in baptismals that'd have our insides in stitches, then say something to hit each of us on our nailhead. *Joey*, she'd tell me, *get up and live. Life's no mystery: stop thinking and love. Love Lara and Renee with your soul's soul. Trace*, she'd say, *thank you for attending me through all this. You're my own baby to kill the blues. Dougie has Jimmy-magic in him. Hold tight to that boy.* She'd talk turkey to everybody about what it's like to be alive, how life has two big hands like a man; the sweet one gives you all the great gifts of a lifetime, and the other is a bone-breaking fist. In this world, who could expect to get one without the other? She'd say *please, please, please don't be sad for me*, and there'd be three exclamation marks after *I love you!!!* Mama'd join O.W. at the head of her own casket. She'd gaze down on herself, touch her cheek the way she did Papa Stepwell's. "I'm sorry, honey," she'd tell herself with all the tenderness of mothers and daughters. My mama'd weep real tears for herself, for us all. Then she'd console O.W., tell him all the good things that had happened between them. She'd touch the scar she'd once clawed into his cheek with the tip of her fingers, the way I'd seen her do so many times when he was ailing. When she'd say *Jimmy*, O.W.'d break a little, and the two of them would embrace and the tears would come and they'd make peace with the difference between what was and what could have been. Flashed before my mother's and father's eyes would be the day they married, how the wide river stretched green and lush through Mom Dee's plate glass window high in the Himalaya House. For a moment I'd be best man again, a breathing link between them, about to say I do.

Maybe it's not the worst thing to forgive, she'd say to O.W. *This, even. Can't we get past this?* And, finally, her last words—*I love you.*

Traceleen's picked out a lily spray so white it hurts here in the Exquisite Farewell Room's directed lighting. People have written their names on the lines in the *Josephine Harvell Memorial Guest Book*, Treadways and Spences and Elliotts, some of them I know from way off like recognizing the scar on a middle knuckle of a finger you once doctored. *Visit the Josephine Stepwell Harvell website for touching online memorials*, we're instructed. Emanating from Mama, fourteen rows of chairs with a walkway down the middle. Some people sit, some people stand, hands stuffed in pockets, talking in little voices. Occasionally somebody laughs, then looks at the floor. Over there's Jimmy's best friend, a pallbearer I haven't seen since the funeral. They went off as missionaries to build Baptist churches in Alaska—him and Jimbo. I've got a picture of them holding this leg-long salmon; Jimmy's got one gill and preacher the other—summer before graduation. He's grown a double chin, preacher, and his wife is pregnant. I picture my brother aged, beholding this room—and it's some fight to wrest that image from my brain. I'd say the walls are bright white, though there's some kind of pink trick in them. And of course the place is windowless, dead center of the funeral home, no sunlight will ever see this space.

"Is MaMa happy in her casket?" Lara points at it. Renee looks petrified, the three of us hold hands.

Behind my back, an uncle on O.W.'s side says, "She'll start coming to you when you dream, you know. That's how it happened to me."

"Is she hungry, Daddy?"

"My own mama lay under for thirty years now. Snap your fingers. I still see her laying in her box, a little girl again."

The flowers have a tuned up, high alert odor. Cold air blows down from vents above and I remember how a high school buddy whose daddy was principal filched keys to the janitor's room beside the girl's athletic dressing room, how he produced these blurry pictures of skin and hair and hip bones against cinderblock walls. People verge between casual and church clothes. The Uncle wears a brown clip-on tie and a suit. "I miss her so bad," he says. "Not a day I don't want to dig her up just to see her face again." He says it to me straight-faced and pats my back, turns to Bold and Judy, begins again.

"I want to see her, Dad."

Renee moves to shield us from Mama's casket.

I lift my daughter to my face, feel her good strong shoulders—swimmers' shoulders, like her mother's. In the moments before we left the beach, the blue-cold Atlantic, the three of us sat on Third Avenue's board rails watching summer-tanned teens surf out the high tide; we didn't speak, a lost world now. "Everything dies, sweetie."

"You?"

I say, "Me."

"Me?"

A guy on my Pony League team once hit me in the head with a number thirty-three aluminum bat during the ninth inning of a tied game with Knight's Knockers. I was on deck, batting clean-up, about to knock sweet Jesus out of anything pitched between numbers and knees. *Ping*, the bat went, heat lightning on a cloudless day. *Ping*, I remember thinking. *Ping*.

"No. Not you ever, sweetie." Between me and Mama, Renee searches faces. In her eyes, I see the moment it happens, the instant when space and time shifts gears. The room goes dead quiet. Blood drains out of faces.

Casketside, O.W. glares down the corridor. Dora—Mama's friend from next door—has just walked in with a squat bearded man, a dwarf or a husky midget. The whole place sees him stand on tiptoes and sign Mama's book. Dora escorts the stranger into the room. *Davey Washer*, though I've never seen him outright, I know my blood uncle straight-away. Mama's told me the stories, sometimes on nights when thunder scared me to her room for the bedtime story of my lineage.

I heard it on the day we finally had it out over Buddy Washer. Renee and I'd flown Mama to Salt Lake that June, and she'd arrived in a freak snow. This was the year the light hurt her eyes, and she wore those wacky wrap-around sunglasses for old people. Lara was five months—a hazel-eyed star of a baby, and Mama took her into her arms, walked out and sat down under the pear in green grass and tried to make an impression that would last beyond the grave. They lay cooing to one another while I hoed a row of bolted spinach, listening to Mama tell Lara the story of her life. That night, she sat with me on the back patio where we could see the white frame bungalow house across our street. Mormons owned it, rented for next to nothing to newly married LDS couples who'd move in and fuck like badgers and promptly conceive a child, give birth and move up to better. The house was entirely whitewashed—bright white—and the streetlight shone on the south wall that glowed the way a pale hand would in deep water.

"You look like Buddy," Mama said out of the blue. "He had the best teeth."

Then, for a while we followed familiar paths, me asking how on earth she could run off with a man like him. She said how she got me out of the deal, and that only a person capable of loving deeply and despite human frailties could ever expect to be happy in this world.

"Did he ever hurt you? My daddy?"

Mama looked at the sad lit house and made a sound like a sigh. She was pretty, even swollen with lupus, and we'd always been on the same track. Her voice—I've read how the unborn hear their mother's voices through the womb, and it resonates inside them forever and ever.

"He took me and his brother Davey out to this canyon. We went barefoot down this deer trail. There were other times."

"Why are you telling me this?"

She was crying, I could hear it in her voice. "How else will you know?"

"So what happened?"

"Nothing. I was afraid he'd hurt me. And I was afraid he'd hurt you."

"Am I like him?"

Lara smiled in Mama's lap, grasped curls, double handfuls of black hair and made bird sounds.

"He stalked us once as a mailman. He'd come to kidnap you."

The saddest light I've ever seen haloed the house across the street. I knew I'd always remember how it was. "You told me he was dead. Remember?"

"I'm sorry," she cried. "*I'm sorry, I'm sorry, I'm sorry.* I can't take this baloney, Joey. You break my heart. What do you want? What do you want me to give you?"

She got up and stumbled through the back door with my daughter in tow, banged her shoulder while climbing the steep steps. The bathroom light flipped on and I could see her outline through the glass, taking the pills, washing them down.

Then the light went out and the sad light washed over the white frame house which was that week being prepared for a new bride and groom. Soon they'd cross the threshold and the curtains would be drawn and it would all begin again. O.W. shakes an elderly woman's hand. His black boots reflect the ceiling's fake light. Davey sits in a folding chair beside Dora as Shurl walks in to direct the viewing ceremony in a mauve dress printed with purple iris. She nods at me, the look on her face neither here nor there. People are taking seats. Anything at all could happen in Lonoke on viewing day. Mama'd know how to run this show. She'd be dressed in white lace with her black hair shining on her shoulders, that wide Stepwell grin, about to repeat O.W.'s *I do.* Behind my back, it happens. The last thing I witness before leaving is the look on my blood uncle's face when the casket gets opened. Behind my back, the image of whatever's five days dead in that box will not bleed into who I am, how I view the world. But my blood uncle, Davey, he sees. On the way out, I recognize myself in his face, the way I could with Jimmy.

24.

Funeral morning, O.W. meets us at the front door, fussing with an IceLand tietack. He's dressed in a dark blue suit that Mama picked out two months back before the surgery that she was convinced would kill her. A Cadillac ticks in the driveway, a black shiny one. It's the sort of morning when, back in Utah, a diamondback will wind cross my path, and when I speak to it, when I say, "Hello brother rattlesnake," the thing'll yawn open its mouth, unfurl fangs and strike the air between us.

"Good morning." Renee says it after a few seconds.

The tie-tack's got both O.W.'s hands. The sun shines in on his face, on the pink scar from the night Mama called out. I smell donuts, black coffee and flowers. He says, "Morning," and I can tell he's seen more of it than me. Tucked in my hind pocket, Mama's eulogy, handwritten at sunrise under the eight-sided hotel gazebo.

"How was it?" I ask. Overnight, I learned that Mama'd appointed Dora to notify folk west of the Mississippi should any harm come her way. This included the Arizona Washers, for whom Davey was the family representative. I keep seeing him, the look on his face when the casket opened.

"Fine," he says. "Come on in."

The living room is dim, though some light's filtering through Mama's bay window. On the couch sits sullen-faced Aunt Mean, Grandpa Stepwell's sister who any second, I can tell, is about to say something awful. Her middle-aged son sits beside her, holding one of his wife's white hands, so they've got the whole wall locked up. A pale man thumbs a black bible. Overhead fly the eternal cargo planes from the Jacksonville base, their cross-shaped shadows hurtling neighborhoods from Gunter's paradise to here.

"How you doing?" I ask.

"Me?" Mean says.

I say, "Yes, ma'am." For the first time in maybe twenty years, the television is turned off, though when I look, it's just that the sound's turned down on the *Praise Channel*, Jimmy Swaggart singing a duet with a woman in blue chiffon.

"Your mama's in heaven now. She's walking with her dead baby this second. Her hurt's all gone you know," Mean says.

I picture Mama and Jimmy on streets of gold. When they took me to his wrecked car, I fished a senior ring out of head-blood pooled in the driver's side floorboard. "Thank you, Aunt Mean."

Tough Man runs out the open door, down Willy Ray, just goes off running. Uncle Bold and Aunt Judy almost clip him when they turn in the drive. They're black-dressed for a funeral. My clothes are a mismatch I'll try to cover with one of O.W.'s Sunday coats, one Mama'd said she wouldn't be seen dead with him wearing, he'll tell me. Everybody's in the living room, my stupid senior picture with my blow-dried hair up on the hall wall, Jimmy's grinning beside me, blue Trace.

"Why aren't you hurting, Joey? Say son?" Mean tilts her head. "Don't a son hurt for its mama?"

"Shut up, Mean," Trace says out of the blue from the kitchen table.

In walks Dora with a yellow squash casserole. "I brought this. Jo loved this. She'd want me to make it for the family." She reaches a Pyrex dish out for me to take. A country woman who hangs snakes from her fruit trees to bring rain, I see her muscling the tree into the hole dug between houses. She smells like cedar.

O.W. says, "Come back here, Joey."

I pass Renee Dora's squash.

"*Now*," he says.

Renee, my wife, I haven't spoken to her for a long time, she's looking at me, gauging me. Lara's eating a donut. Who talks with their four year old about what's inside a casket? She'll never know my people now.

"Joey," O.W. says. He motions with his eyes.

Dora's eyelids narrow. "You hang tough," she tells me.

I follow him down the hall, toward Mama's bedroom, Traceleen's abandoned room on the opposite side of the hall of the master room where O.W. sleeps when he's not out on the recliner. The hall's lined with the framed high points of our lives together: weddings, candles being blown out at birthday parties, Jimmy smiling in a top hat and white tuxedo at Senior Prom—the good times Mama needed to witness again and again as she struggled from bed to hot tub and back to bed. Probably our hallway was like every other hallway on Willy Ray Street. We held no monopoly on fucked-upedness, surely we didn't. O.W. opens Mama's door. It's real dark inside, I can't see a thing. "This stuff needs looking through," he tells me.

"Today?"

"So you'll know what's here."

"What's here?"

To my surprise, the big old man starts to cry, and he looks like Jimmy for a second, so that I wonder if he was like my brother once, just a sweet kid, about to get the ride of his life—is that what Mama fell in love with? "I tried to call her," he says. "I've always dreaded calling in the afternoon and getting no answer."

"What happened?"

"I wish that bitch would leave." He nods back up the hall. "I have to tell you something. Mama'd want me to tell you."

I'm face to face with O.W. For years I dreamed myself grown up enough to kill him. I could throttle him this second, I could try. Isn't that what it's all about, kill your daddy and take Mama back? *I do, I do, I do*—the nursery room needle caught, skipping in the grooves of time? Even if Buddy Washer has somehow made the drive with Davey, dressed up as whatever the fuck, we have no history together, no trace. Like it or no—O.W.'s the one. We're standing at the doorway. Up in the living room, the pale-faced man's reading *I have a new commandment, that ye love one another as I have loved you.* My father's face is straight in front of mine, his blue eyes very much aware of me, of the moment, of our shared story, everything: all that time on the road to think, to reinvent the world he willed.

"Your real father's dead, son."

My eyes are adjusting—Mama's bed's a mess.

"Buddy Washer. That midget told me last night."

I see a postman cursing us from the backseat of a cop car spewing gravel: *son of a bitch, son of a bitch*. Out of my mouth, "That son of a bitch is nobody to me."

The wall dusts O.W.'s shoulder. "I'm sorry. Talk to the little man. Family's family."

"Aren't you my goddamn family?" I think to hit him in the face, but instead brush the dust off his shoulder.

The look is as solemn as has ever been on a solemn man's face. He says, "Will you help me?" His IceLand tietack's upside down—I've never one time seen him tie a tie in his life. For all his life, surely, it was Mama tying his ties. At our wedding, we wore twin clip-ons.

I take one tongue in each hand, separate and match them, stick the tietack needle through the thick middle. "What happened to Mama?"

O.W. nods. "The coroner's report will say accidental drowning. But she had a heart attack. The insurance people won't pay if it doesn't say accidental."

"How can you know that?"

He wipes one big hand on the other. I've watched him lie to Mama a hundred times, straight-faced, without a twitch. He measures me. "I'm smarter than you'll ever be," he screamed at me once from his recliner, a rerun of Gomer Pyle going on a sad-hot afternoon when the refrigerator'd gone out and the whole house reeked of rotten hamburger. Then he got up and carved a soapbox derby car for my Cub Scouts meet. What the fuck?

"We've had four days now, Joey. Me and Trace. That's enough."

He's on one side of Mama's dark doorway, I'm on the other. In the hallway with both of us dressed up again, darkening the full-length mirror he's screwed to the end wall. Just like before, her between us. Life is the brute and the healer, Mama'd say. All my life I'd dreamed of breaking O.W.'s bones, of knocking teeth out of his head—and what kind of way was that for a son to think about its daddy? Once Renee asked, "How on *earth* can you love that man?" and the edge of my defense shocked. "How's it possible to love anybody?" I demanded. And the question stands—do we love *because* or *despite*? Dumb truck driver or the snake emboldened, why love? What do I know? Mama's dead, and that feels like the world. "Can I ask you something? O.W.?"

He says, "Sure."

"What's woodpussy?"

"What?"

"Woodpussy." Up the hall Lara's laughing, and I hear Tough Man's little dog paws clicking on the kitchen floor. Somebody's chased Mama's little dog down and brought it home. "That day we fought, when I broke your tooth, you called me woodpussy. What's that?"

The solemn look melts, and he's just him again, O.W., a man who'd given Mama a loaf of white bread on the day they met. He says it, "Woodpussy."

"Yeah."

"Remember all those antelope? That place I took you, Highway 80 outside Rawlins?"

"Where the truck rolled uphill."

"There's this aspen grove up on a hilltop I drove through once. Somebody's carved these tree burls into pussy-shaped things that leak red sap. Like a woman on her period. They look like the real deal. Weirdest things you've ever seen, woodpussies."

25

Inside, the closet door's broken, and the clothes rod's collapsed; all her clothes are piled in a heap like they've died too. I draw the blind so bright light comes in through the dirty glass.

Tough Man has shit three times on the window side of the bed where I step, dust from the ceiling fan filtering down. The peanut butter and jelly sandwich is half eaten on the night stand. Her bed and every other available surface in the room is loaded with hospital bills and prescriptions and insurance papers and letters from Washington, D.C., The Democratic National Convention, knickknacks from Las Vegas casinos and empty picture frames, tax records and romance novels, pagemarked with pictures of Lara, an old mother's day card, the program from Aunt Peg's funeral, the room is noisy with Mama's perpetual effort to drive away chaos while creating all the more. She wasn't planning on dying—that much is for sure. Calendars flap open on the bed, dresser and floor. Blue Cloud, our Fourth of July vacation is marked in big red letters, as well as dates for the rest of the month and year—everybody's birthdays and Christmas gift ideas. On the date when one of Jimmy's friends died is printed a reminder to send the parents a note: *we never lose the ones we love, we keep them in our hearts.*

A list of phone numbers with my name, Renee and Lara, a big heart drawn around us. Christmas cards and dirty socks in the mix, orange wedges and chewing gum wrappers—this is what it's like to be sick. How she could reason at all in the midst of this is a miracle.

Thirteen copies of Elvis Sings Gospel on CD, stacked beside Jimmy's silver pistol on the night stand. And beneath that, just off to the side away from the bed, Mama's fake leather briefcase with its little three-digit-combination lock and double fake brass latches. It sits in a cleaned out spot, the only dustless thing inhabiting my mother's life. Lupus got her forced into retirement from the state a few years earlier—this was her work briefcase, what she took on trips to conventions in big cities—San Diego, Chicago, Atlanta—hotels with views, good lighting, happy hour hors d'oeuvres and jazz on the veranda. Places away from O.W.

Inside an organizer notebook I find about thirteen unofficial variations of her last will and testament, and a draft of her funeral service, planned out in detail before the last operation. She was sure that was the big one and had mailed everyone she knew last letters, farewell sweetnesses; to Lara she sent a talking photo of her and O.W. that repeated Mama saying *I love you, I love you, I love you.* Lara'd scotch taped the button down and the thing said its love all night long until it malfunctioned and went mute. The scar tissue in Mama's abdomen had blocked a stomach artery, though the docs all said that in her state, going under was a big risk, that she should get her life in order. So she did. We got phone calls and emails and notes. One box overflowed with faded spring jonquils and dogwood leaves. Pictures of forsythia in the snow. I'm convinced she reached out to everyone that way, maybe even Shawn Terrence Lord off in California who'd turned his back when I snapped the picture, his curly hair falling down over his collar. Mama'd insured herself to the bone, and she had her state retirement and Medicare; cash was to be set aside for each grandchild, college funds, a modest inheritance for each of us. "Let Joey speak for the family," one draft says, along with names and numbers for all the pallbearers. She lists songs—Willy Nelson "Angel Flying Too Close to the Ground." ZZ Top, for some crazy reason, and Bonny Raitt singing "Angel From Montgomery" and "Too Long at the Fair." She requests "Amazing Grace," the old number I heard sung when they lowered Mama Stepwell, and later Jimmy, down into the ground and we all stood there on Astro Turf saying *I once was lost but now I'm found, was blind but now I see.* Through her window, the light is fierce.

Her briefcase's three-digit combination is nothing—it pops smack open with one pry from a fingernail file, the latch snapping the way a mousetrap goes off behind a chest freezer. I smell her. And I feel for all the world like she's trying to tell me something this second, that this instant is crucial, somehow, in understanding who I am, and what I come from and where I'll be going and how it will be for Lara, even. I'm to move slowly, to be alert to what I'm doing. I drink deep from the water bottle on the night stand. It's cold and good and I remember how Mama craved icewater, was always getting up for a drink in the dark. The contents of the briefcase are carefully arranged, which surprises me because Mama usually let things lay where they fall. But not here—there's a set order, a clear rhyme and reason—call it a progression: Razorback tickets, an invitation to Oaklawn courtesy of Governor Jim Guy Tucker, office briefs and legislative notes, two letters from me and a big sloppy heart Lara drew for last Valentine's. Pictures from Traceleen's prom, the one she attended the day after Jimmy died with Stumpy Stumpfield who'd asked her at the last minute—my sister manages a smile; a Cohiba cigar scotchtaped to a piece of vellum on which she's written *Election night, November 5, 1996, Little Rock, Arkansas. Cuban cigar shared with our friend and newly re-elected President, Bill Clinton. Love, Mama*; and beneath all this, down past the breath mints and ID badges and dried mother's day corsages, under the insurance settlement papers and the bank notes with O.W.'s name crossed off the accounts, down on the very bottom of it all are letters written in Shawn Terrence Lord's flowery hand, postmarked from San Diego and Dallas and Ft. Lauderdale and Barcelona, Spain— one of which I scan long enough to know what they all say, how it goes.

The letters line up chronologically—they've been read and thought about. Beneath Lord's letters, stacked domino style across the bottom of Mama's briefcase, envelopes bulge with photographs from Jamaica and Washington, D.C. and the Little Rock inauguration—big, glossy western size prints of Mama and Shawn Lord drinking fruit drinks with umbrellas on a white sand beach. Lord in a workout room, straining under a bench press. In dinner dress, they pose with Hillary Clinton and the woman from Little Rock who starred in that movie *An Officer and a Gentleman*, whoever she is. A dim-lit run, maybe three photos, show Lord in red bikini underwear, on a hotel bed, his legs spread out and a come-to-me look on his face. I tear this photo to pieces and those pieces into pieces, shove it all into my pants pocket where an unwrapped cough drop has melted.

I shut and lock my mother's briefcase and put it back exactly where it was before, in the cleaned away spot beside the table where the peanut butter and jelly sandwich attracts tiny fruit flies. I shut Mama's door, pull hard so the doorframe squeals and the bolt clicks and I walk away, up past my own old bedroom where I'd lay on the floor on afternoons after house framing or finishing concrete and dream up schemes for getting the fuck out of Arkansas forever. Sunburned, I'd lie there on the carpet with the sounds of my family going on outside, in summer time, the cool air whirring through the air conditioner vent, and when the sun went down, the night noise, and somebody'd wreck their scooter just over the train tracks across town, and I'd hear Mama and Daddy laugh at something and Jimmy'd walk through the hall from his back bedroom, back past the washer and dryer by the garage door, and O.W.'d razz him about a hot date or the beard he'd grown that summer. Or sometimes Traceleen would just die to play us all a song on her cassette player, and it would be a bubblegum love medley and we'd all crack up and have supper at the table where O.W.'d pray, and we'd all hold hands, then eat chili or spaghetti or hamburger stroganoff steaming on the table. Outside, these big intense spider webs stretched, twenty yards from one end to the other, gleaming under the pear and apple trees. O.W.'d say Amen, and Mama'd look up, and we'd see each other and know that this was right, and EMTs would attend the man who'd wrecked his scooter on the train track, take his pulse, check for internal bleeding and O.W. would say Amen. Our future was deep with hope, all good things were surely headed our way there on Willy Ray Street in the delta with its pure gold earth. And then a rabbit would squeal and cargo planes rattled the glass fixtures and one of us would flip on the TV and O.W.'d take to the recliner and Beach Blanket Bingo would just be starting on Saturday Matinee. Our lives moved forward.

Up through the hallway I see Renee, Lara in her lap, on the loveseat beside the fireplace where Mama's picture—the one from the viewing—has been propped up against the glass beside the gold poker and shovel. Brother Dell's nowhere to be seen. Uncle Bold's outside smoking with Aunt Judy. Traceleen's out there, with her little big boy, Douglas. Mean and her son are sour-faced, somebody's got their goats. A car is being sent this second, a long black limo from the funeral home, the one the monkey man'd been laying the shine to when Shurl explained the four days of the human body. When the woodpecker blazed high in a hickory, hammering its way between the living and the dead. A horse had neighed—people drove by on the highway, going down the road with their radios on, singing bubblegum love songs and cracking up—the world turning.

And here's O.W., my adoptive father, his tietack straight now, a dead serious look on his face, only merged with something I can't quite get right in my head. Mama lorded over him for thirty years. She'd been boss, all through it all, the divorces, separations, and even that night when she screamed out for help. *He* was the one that came out with his cheek laid open from one of her fingernails. "Never be like him," she told me the day after, him gone to drive a truck full of chilled feeder pigs. Before the last operation, the one they both believed would kill her, she'd picked out this fierce blue suit for her funeral. Out of dozens, this's the one she'd settled on. She chose the dress she's wearing this instant, chilled in the white casket that rocks gently toward us.

Only, the operation didn't kill her. She got *better*. And the money came through. And they'd planned it all out, down to the shade of her lipstick and the socks he was wearing. She'd come to her senses, known she'd need the money for care, maybe even planned to move out. Mama'd cut O.W. off, and he took that as a betrayal—pure and simple.

And what on earth, a man photographed in red underwear?

Mama was in charge, just like she'd finally been with Buddy Washer. Just like she took charge of her part in the campaign that brought us together for the inauguration in D.C., where Shawn Lord had turned his back on me before the swearing-in ceremony. Jamaica and Ocho Rios and who knows where else were documented by her studied eye back in the briefcase, with its flimsy latch that any dipshit with a fingernail file could pop.

Nothing is simple. Nothing. What I can tell you is this: when your mother dies, even if she's been sick for a long time, even if you fear something awful's been done to her, even if she told you that she was going to die and you agreed to deliver the eulogy at her funeral service, even if you've thought out the words during winter happy hours—there is no getting ready, no thinking that can ever get you ready for the moment when the monkey man drives into your driveway in that long black car, how everything is on the verge of something else, endless not-knowing in the face of absolute knowing. The edges of the ripped up photograph dig into me through my pants pocket—my life.

And together we make an entourage, the monkey man at the helm, wheeling under the blue sky and the heat and the daffodil.

26.

Consider the First Baptist Church: the leviathan girth and height of its whitewashed steeple threatening at any second to flip the whole block upside down. The new wing, a brother Dellwood T. Walker production, is diamond-shaped, mutating out of the former sanctuary hall onto Cherry Street. The red brick bleeds down the street, into the new metal diamond where the architect has opted for a windowless experience with the holy ghost. Light's iffy—why take chances with light? Better the dark backlit than the unpredictability of sunshine. The *Committee for Righteousness Sake* last year joined hands with the *Society of the Just Made Perfect* to purchase then tear down all the low rent units on Cherry's south side. They plowed the duplexes and the church gymnasium—which doubled as a cafeteria for Wednesday night potlucks—under for a jumbo parking lot, cut up by yellow lines. Each parking spot sports a number corresponding to the family's tithe; a sweet offering won a shorter walk across the hot asphalt which made for withered corsages and sweaty arm pits. The Kentucky Blue Grass surrounding the structure is doing quiet well, thank you, with only the faintest whiff of tick spray from Deacon Ringgold's Bug Stompers operation, provided free of charge monthly for lucky number thirteen on the steaming black lot.

And *oh* if this place could talk, this First Baptist Church of Lonoke, Arkansas, what stories it could tell. It would no doubt recount how, when in its infancy back when the century past was itself still a baby, the mayor and town council gathered here to castrate Carl Jenkins—how dare he move his black-ass family into these city limits, like his shit didn't stink. Hadn't Brother Dellwood's own granddaddy been there at the altar breathing a prayer, the curved-bladed knife slick in its leather scabbard? Surely, if the place could speak, it would recall the lone devotionals between pastor and school girl, the doe-eyed ones who stared at their feet for the rest of their days. Lord Jesus, should this building put tongue to its history, wouldn't it pay a word or two to the choir loft where so many Directors have led young men through the hardships of fully opening up to the holy spirit; where they opened up their mouths to the glorious flow of praise and rapture? All those marryings and buryings, would not this fine old sanctuary have cause to thank its Royal Ambassador Sunday School Teachers for their missionary work, for implanting the word in heathen ears, how they'd reached out to brother and sister churches throughout the three-B triangle of Butlerville, Beebe and Bayou Meto. Had not they multiplied God's kingdom on earth? All the great sinners and great sins perpetrated and forgiven on bended knees down at the heavy oak pulpit, would they not merit consideration, sins of such weight they remain hard to speak, even for a church gifted with the tongues of angels? Hadn't the guilt-ridden souls reaped what they'd sewed? All the baggage of the here and now, how flesh smacks its lips, how it convicts. What was this life anyway but a shade compared to the hereafter? Better to just get done with it—*Paradise* is waiting. Where the sick will be well and the one-legged walk and the stutterer speak and the drunkard be sober and the adulterer be pure and all will be made holy by the savior who loved so that he bled his own blood, *hallelujah, thine be the glory.* Should this place speak in the language of men, what would it have to say about our treacherous hearts? If the church, like Brother Dellwood says, is a living, breathing thing, I wonder what it would discern about what brings us here today? I mean, these Mormons I live with in Utah, they've got this Doctrine of Blood Antonement practiced by an order called the *Dannites.* These guys go by the rule that it's the most supreme form of love to kill a sinner and then, after their soul's turned loose, baptize them in the name of Jesus and so send them on to heaven. The seeming breach of the First Commandment is justified by no less than eternal bliss in heaven. Take the word *Baptist,* which comes from *baptism,* isn't that all just about dying to get reborn? The bridegroom is prepared for the bride and the church prepares itself for the sinful mortal—take this and drink, it is my blood; take this and eat, it is my flesh—and even the meekest among us cannibals parts lips for the godhead.

Brother Dellwood T. Walker stands with one hand on Mama's fierce white casket. He sees me the moment I enter and smiles that slight smile so we both know what's what. The spray my sister's chosen is overwhelming in its whiteness, lilies I know now, punctuated by a single red rose with the stem cut short to symbolize Jimmy's life, and what will become the thematic for the day, how Mama's gone this day to walk with her beloved son in heaven, *Amen*. Lara and Renee are beside me, we walk down the steeply falling middle aisle. The room's dark and cavernous, with a jumbo-screen teletron mounted up on the ceiling with the salvation score set at thirty-three. Shurl is here, directing traffic. That fifth-day look—I see it in her eyes. She motions us into the family pew. Mama's photo grins at us from beside the casket and the odor of flowers starts to get me. For the first time, I understand why flowers and death go hand in hand; I'd missed the whole masking thing with Jimmy.

These new pews are cushioned. Family Row is dead in front of the casket where my mother lay—unimaginably—on crushed velvet. I shake the image from my head and scoot to the far end, as much distance as I can put between us and where Brother Dell stands in his Baptist preacher version of O.W.'s Jim Ed Brown Mensware suit. People fan out in all directions—some I recognize from Mama's office in Little Rock, and relatives whose faces are strangely familiar, Mama's oldest friends from school days, people from the campaign circle, stray men who could be anybody at all, and a whole pewful of black folk in colorful suits and dresses. Sad-sad organ music rolls over us. I wish for light.

I'm not a prayer—not really—but maybe I'm thinking that if grace exists, let a truckful of it rain down on me and my wife and daughter and Traceleen and O.W. and Mama there where she lay. Next to my heart, in the breast pocket of O.W.'s coat, Mama's eulogy.

I've confided in no one that, for some days now, I've mixed the funeral up with a wedding. Since the moment Renee shook me awake, five days ago now, I've held myself together and tried my goddamndest to do right. My lifetime has revisited me; some dots connect and some don't—maybe some are connected that aren't supposed to be, I don't know. The bloody history and the history of my blood. I don't know. I know.

One day soon, the events that have led up to this moment in my history will coalesce. And it will be no consolation. My mother is dead. My *mother* is *dead*.

Her body is in that casket this second, dressed in the dress she picked out with her own eyes and imagined on her own dead body—she's pictured the dress on her dead body and that's a place I'll never go.

Brother Dell stands there with his hand splayed on her cold casket like he owns it, looking me straight in the face, thinking that I'm the same punk-fuck he once Cain and Abled, but that's not so, and that I know this means all. Mama knew it from the beginning, where this was all going, how it would come down, and still she fought like a tiger, and there's something to be said for going down swinging. Forever people will stab you in the back, the very genes we're made of necessitate self-interest and viciousness and survival no matter what—that's what life means: *live, no matter what.* Others argue for inherent benevolence–the power of love. And if there's any transcendence in these strange, strange lifetimes we keep on living, it is all about love, the lone buoy in a sea of death. *Love* or *death*, take your pick.

The preacher takes three steps up onto the podium, sits down on the bench facing us and nods his head at me. The music quits. I step up into the vacuum of false light, past Mama's casket and up to the pulpit where I look into the sea of faces and unfold Mama's eulogy. The mike whistles when I touch it, Brother Dell's eyes burn into my back.

My daughter looks straight at me through my mother's face—how on earth to explain this to a four-year-old child. How on earth to explain anything at all to anybody, really. The silence is down on us. Breaths are being held in chests where hearts beat. Before the last operation, the one Mama and Daddy believed would kill her, Mama sent the talking photo of her and O.W. with a bright flash on their faces and happy grins. "I love you, Lara," Mama said. "I love you, Lara," Daddy said. Only Lara somehow erased the voices, so when you pushed the button, nothing happened. Renee retaped the I love yous in her own voice, alien and downright funny out of O.W.'s mouth, but dead on for Mama. Lara never knew the difference.

I meet O.W.'s eyes—ice blue in this light.

Off to the right, sitting on the edge of the wood pew, my blood Uncle Davey with his hands in his lap. When Renee was pregnant with Lara, I'd been afraid we'd birth a dwarf. It was possible, dwarves were in my blood. In person, my blood Uncle seems like anybody else, flesh and blood. Beside him, Dora's swishing a folding fan, just like in the movies of southern funerals where somebody's about to breakdown and jump into the casket or shoot their first cousin.

"A while back," I say, and the collective breath of this space is released, "Mama asked me to speak at her funeral. She believed I could say what needed to be said."

In back of the dark room, the double doors swing open for a second so I can see actual light. A man enters, I can't tell who. Trace, my one sister, is sobbing. I feel for her—at least the sad organ's shut up.

"So here I am.

"My name is Joey Harvell, Josephine's oldest. I'm honored. Can I ask that everybody please stand up, please."

A few jaws drop and Brother Dellwood clears his throat behind my back. O.W. stiffens—he's so close, I could reach out and tap him with a stick.

"She was sick. Mama hurt bad for a long time. Please stand on up."

One by one everyone who's not a Baptist rises. Uncle Bold and Aunt Judy rise, along with Dora and Davey and the score of black folk—Mama's Little Rock friends. They rock back and forth on their heels, maybe sense the threat of jubilation in the air. The first of what will become looks of monumental confusion begin. The man in the back of the hall is standing.

"Lupus didn't kill her. Thank you. Stand on up."

Behind me, the years and years where trucks roll uphill and postmen and dead little boys in sailor suits, painted ducks and museum mummies. The howl of tornadoes and thunder and dream fire. Before me, my mother and my family and all these faces between me and the double doors that will open again to the world where fish leap house high and a solitary youth paddles out a riptide.

"What I'm saying is that Mama didn't lose her fight. I can prove it."

People swivel heads, swallow, look quizzically at the salvation score on the jumbo screen teletron. The pallbearer who's a cop checks his watch.

"Yesterday I talked with some of you here right now.

"One of you said, 'These last few weeks, Josie'd call me once a day and ask for her laugh fix.' I'd say, 'Well which one should we talk about first, the preacher or the deacons,' and we'd laugh till we cried.'"

Maybe the man who entered late is Shawn Terrence Lord, whose puzzle pieces are entirely reconstructable in my pocket. Maybe he's not afraid of O.W. anymore and is ready to turn his face full to the light, let himself be seen the way Mama saw him. Maybe Lord can speak to Mama's capacity to love? I'd like to slap his ass just as bad as O.W.'s. The hell with Davey too. Who'd he think he was, showing up when I was forty years old?

"And another one said, 'I was in love with her. Everybody was. She's the best damn dancer in Lonoke County.' Stand up. Raise your hands in the air."

Behind me, Brotherl Walker, *That's a-nuf*, he says.

"How is it then, I'd like to ask, that my mama, Josephine Harvell, gets remembered? Say? For a salty joke about Baptist preachers and deacons? What kind of wife was she? What kind of mother? Swollen, bleeding inside. Say?"

"*Say*," a voice from somewhere in front of me.

"I was with her at Bill Clinton's inauguration. People were dancing after, and before I knew it Mama had the center of the floor with this real tall man named Lord."

"*Lordy-man*," a dark lady sings.

"The film crews rolled up these huge cameras and got it all on tape for the late news. Mama dancing. And she saw me looking at her and held out a hand for me to join and I did. Honey—I remember her saying *Go!*"

Now, many in the congregation sense something off—this isn't how it's supposed to go. Funerals aren't like this. Baptists don't dance. We don't make jokes at funerals; we feel guilty, we cry, we tear hair and want to climb into the casket and be the sorry sucks Brother Dell said we were. Brother Dell—the spiraling vortex of his darkness very real behind me.

"Lupus didn't kill her," I say. "She beat that. I'm talking for her now. She outdanced that son of a bitch. She danced all night. She's smoke on the water. She's still dancing. I see her this second. She's dancing in light. Her hips are moving. She's forgiving. She holds the Lord man till he cries."

O.W.'s red-faced. I don't know what I'm doing. My daughter's on her feet, Renee, sister Trace.

"Praise God," one of the African-American ladies says. "Say it!" says another.

Renee's mouth is trembling—the thing is on her now. We meet eyes—I'm crazy, Stepwell crazy, half dwarf. The hysteria is on us, forsythia blooming in her hazel eyes, we could get the sickness this second, laugh our ways to kingdom come. I shut my eyes, let fly, "You can't *hurt* me. You can't *kill* me. You can't *drown* me." Red sparks fly up against my lids. "I'm love. You can't make me hate you. I'm on fire. *I* love you! I *love* you! I love *you!*"

Somebody says, Dear God.

"Jesus," the black lady sings. "Thank you."

"Mama says *love*," I say.

"Love!" the black lady sings.

Love.

Love, somebody's singing.

Go love. I say, *Go love*, and it's done.

When I turn back, Brother Dell's eyes smolder. He spits, steps past me and slaps the mike three times hard. "Be seated," he says. "Order. Order in the Lord's court."

Renee's choked back the laughing sickness, though I wish for the single moment, as I slide onto the pew between her and Lara, that we could all turn lose. I wish we could laugh and sing and dance and praise Mama's lifetime, let love rise up and shake this somber roof. I want to make a joyful noise—how it should be. I clasp my wife's hand and so trembles the energy between us. My parting shot is a taped rendition of, "I'll Fly Away," a full-gospel tune that makes the sorry air thrum, so I hear many toes tapping.

The rest of the service is twisted around the twin notions that Mama's walking in heaven with her *good* dead son, and that the rest of us are likely to die any second and spend eternity in hellfire. Best to renounce Satan and the sins of lust and gluttony and wickedness. We must rededicate ourselves to Christ. We sing sad songs about dying and I sit there watching my daughter write her name on the *Call to Worship* sheet. Then Shurl goes up and stands by Brother Dell and they make ready to open the casket for the last viewing. Renee and Lara and I file back up the steep middle aisle from whence we came, past all the faces now tearstreaked and shaken with grief, past the place where the man I couldn't name had sat, on through the unsealed double doors, into the foyer with its big clear vase full of daffodils set on a table marked *Receiving*.

I search the sign-in sheet for names that ring a bell, think to walk outside and see who's leaving, though all that will have to wait for another day. I'm here now entirely—nothing else matters.

When it's all said and done, we're a little lost, the three of us—Renee, my good wife to whom I've not spoken six sensible words since it started, Lara, who has just asked—in the sweetest sad voice—if Grandma was hungry in her casket, and me—Joey Stepwell Harvell, a man who's just chosen his mother's ghost face over the one people now view. We're lost because the rest of the family, all the Stepwells and Harvells, O.W., Traceleen, Uncle Bold and Aunt Judy, Shurl's whisked them out to the three black hearses where everyone sweats and wipes their foreheads. Through the foyer glass, we see all, but the place is a labyrinth—a mystery—and getting out requires changing levels.

In the stairwell, halfway to the bottom floor, we run into Dora and my Uncle Davey, whose voice I've never heard. "I'd know you anywheres," he says, holds out a ring-studded hand to shake. My blood uncle offers a hand and I take it. "Your old man, he'd be proud of you, son."

"I don't know you."

"Yes, you do," he says, shakes his head and walks up three stairs so we're the same size. "Sometime when this is over, I'll catch up with you," he says. "I got a lot to pass your way. You too, cutie."

Renee puts her arm around my shoulders. The stairwell between floors is heavy with perfume. Dora follows Davey. "Your Mama said she had a soul mate, and it was you." She pats me three times on the shoulder of O.W.'s coat. "There's a man you talked about today—Lord. I called him, too. Josie told me he danced like hell on wheels."

In the hallway out, pallbearers carry the white casket by its silver hardware. The thing looks jet-like, a 747.

"You want his number?" Dora asks.

"No."

The casket freezes Lara.

"We'll be home soon," Renee says and sobs and the three of us hug. We lift Lara up and hug. But my daughter's eyes lock on the casket—the great mystery. "Baby, we'll be all through this soon," Renee says into the side of my face, and I can feel the wet of her lips. Her father's birthday—Cap's 70th—Mama wouldn't have pulled this for all the world, not in a million years. "I'll drive," Renee says. "We're not riding in the car with that man."

O.W. and Brother Dell walk through the doors together. Both see us at the same time. "Bless you, son," the preacher says, his hands laced behind his back. "Bless you."

Renee snaps up Lara and I watch her walk away, out the doors, toward the far off spot in the hot lot where our Silver Pathfinder sits, sought now via missing vehicle reports from Florida to Memphis.

Dell disappears and I'm left with O.W. We walk together, and I follow when he makes a right into the Men's.

We each take a urinal and face the white wall like the one Mama once screamed at me through—*get help, Joey, he's killing me.* No getting away from that—those words, her plea. But he'd been her caretaker as well, her odd caretaker. No doubt, he'd opened the briefcase, maybe during the operation, after Mama had him try on all those suits then Xed his name off the bank accounts and insurance policies. He'd seen into Mama's briefcase. He had surely held in his own hands the photograph of Shawn Terrence Lord that is now ripped up in my pants pocket, evidence that I've now destroyed. There's more. Maybe he'd carefully wiped his fingerprints off all those pictures, gone down to the camera store and bought one of those special rags and those white gloves they use to handle delicate film. He'd seen Mama's lover with that look on his face—kicked back on the hotel bed in bikini underwear. The letters, *sentence* after *sentence.* And covering all the carefully cleaned photographs in Mama's briefcase, my own prints now, carefully set down in tbe bedroom's one clear spot, under the night table where a peanut butter and jelly sandwich rotted. How long has he held this in his heart?

I piss beside my father at the Baptist Church urinal.

"What do you think?" I ask.

O.W. shakes his head, smiles a sheepish smile—the moment we've rocketed toward our whole lives. "I always knew this would happen."

"What?"

O.W. shakes his head side to side, the sheepish smile.

"That I'd have to pee before driving out to that blasted cemetery. And stand here and not be able to."

And that was that. In the shock of looking backwards, the fall is hardest, when cool air comes down from Canada and Mama'd call me and say she was remembering the autumn when I burst through the mouth of the paper jackrabbit, then ran for 275 yards against the Bauxite Pirates. She'd call in fall, when the air got brisk—and in her voice I'd hear the language of my heart.

Part Three

27.

Barely home, we head west. When the highway runs into the Pacific Ocean, we find ourselves in Astoria, Oregon, at the mouth of the Columbia River Gorge— the Mississippi of the Northwest. Windsurfers carve blue waters that bewildered explorers for half a millennium—the sought-after northern passage seeming to possess the gift of making itself invisible. Cape Disappointment the place is called, where we begin the second week of July, 2002, a little less than a month after my mother has drowned and been buried in the ground where a stone with her name on it will be set in fall. By the time we hit the coastal bridges—these architectural works of art in steel and stone—I've run out of dry earth to run away on.

Rivers named Klaskanine, Lewis and Clark, Nehatem, and Sixes pass through fishing villages with blue-painted doors and where you can walk right down to a boat and pay five dollars for a red-fleshed king salmon that saw the sun rise that very day. Natives here worship the fish as a god—fish totems appear in a curve of highway that looks out on rocky islands where seals and sea lions flounce and holler. The air is honest with salt and chill. Someone has told Renee that this place is good medicine, that peace can be made here. My daughter's learned how to write the word love—and I find it when I least expect it, just out of blue sky, like the continuing questions about people in caskets: do they get cold? Do they need *blankies*? Our hotel's plate glass window looks out on the pier with its rickety floorboards stepping out and out into the ocean, a strange ladder out into Cape Disappointment where Vasco DeGama swamped his finest schooner. He'd dared the Columbia's treacherous mouth and lost; the site became a symbol for all the failures of his lifetime—Cape Disappointment—that's the story.

This morning, a fine bright windswept and chilly Monday, we're touring the Astoria Maritime Museum at water's edge. The place documents, among other things, the history of Astoria's canneries which once supplied the world's salmon. Photographs show how hip-booted men smoked cigars and hauled in nets sagging with silver fish, tons of them dragged straight out of the surf with mule teams and then pick-up trucks. Up to the slaughterhouses and canneries where generations of women packed the natives' water god into tin cans. Year after year, Astoria men caught the Jesus out of the fish. The whole world glutted on Oregon salmon— then the fish disappeared. Soon the men had to take to boats and fishing vessels, which meant crossing the killer river's mouth. The fishermen's memorial here lists thousands of drowned souls. And that's what they call them—*drowned souls*.

We view a film that narrates the invention of the Astoria Rescue Vessel, the unflippable lifesaving boat that's saved the lives of fishers from sixty countries. Outside, wafting side to side at low tide, a large rescue ship sits with flags unfurled. Renee buys tickets and we walk the planks down into the metal hull, through the door and into the lifeboat's cramped quarters.

"It smells like a ship. This is always how it is."

Lara's climbing stairs, bouncing on an off-limits bunk.

Renee says, "Like something's burned. Ships all smell this way."

Outside again, wind in our faces, the list of rescues is staggering. We stand there in the wind reading name after name—all the souls who'd crewed the ships named for women. The rescue ship's pulpit bow is a full-breasted mermaid. I see her swimming to men who breathe prayer into water. No Harvells or Stepwells, Renee's finger finds a lone Rockerson.

We hit a fish and chips joint for coffee and head south. 101 skirts the ocean, along massive forests of spruce and pine and redwood that grow right down the craggy cliffs where walls of mussel, clam and starfish shine. Every quarter mile we turn a curve and look out onto a stretch of desolate ocean, these cathedral rock islands in the sun, sights we've not prepared to see. I steer while Renee and Lara *ooh* and *ah*. The coast seems at once lush and stripped to the bone. Bicyclists in blaze-orange backpacks pedal slowly on the roadside. Our radio says that four hundred miles from here, in California, the Redwood forest has caught fire.

We sight the first whales off Cape Meares. The gleaming breaths blow twenty feet high then vanish. The first few times we think we're seeing things, then a silvery breath rises again. One must see a living whale blow many times to be convinced, their breath ghosting the horizon.

We camp at Cape Lookout, just outside Tillamook, where I buy a pawnshop surf rod, pick up hooks and lead and a package of frozen bait that falls apart as soon as it thaws. I find oysters at a shack on the bay near the woods, where a woman in a flowery dress bakes bread. "Here," she says straight away when Lara and I walk through the door. "I like these." The floor is flour-dusted with footprints. "Take one, honey," she says to Lara, holding out a steaming muffin. I order two-dozen fresh oysters, lemons and butter.

"My MaMa's not hungry in her casket," Lara says.

The woman looks at me, deep into me with brown eyes. All day long I've been meeting people that look at me this way, like they know who I am, the person I've forgotten being. She smiles a little and I see her slip three extra oysters into our clear bag.

"I sure hope not, sweetie." She hands me the shellfish, the sea grass they're wrapped in shining bright green. I carry out the scent of bread and water, the vision of my daughter with the sun on her cheek, eating the buttered muffin, the sea spread out behind her while we drive.

There's rain in the morning, then the sun is out, a chill wind. I wear river shorts, wake Lara, and the two of us carry the surf rod and a cooler out to low tide, walk a half-mile down through pools of sea anemone and starfish, these fantastic reds and blues. We're barefoot, looking out over the surf southwest, the sun rising behind our backs, warm already, though this wind is a knife. I peel another fleece from the backpack and put it on Lara.

Three Chinese men in full waders and storm parkas, wooly caps pulled tight over their heads, surf-fish the second breaker, a hundred yards or more out in the cold shallow water. They're good casters, all three, but the one on the south, he's in a zone. We sit cross-legged on the beach and watch, my own rod leaned against the cooler and my daughter in my lap, breathing, eyes full open, nighttime on her breath. And this Chinese man who's in a zone, I watch him bait and cast a double rig just like I use for Blues, trot three strides into a wave and let fly, the lead and hook and bait zinging fifty, sixty yards out to the splash. He tightens up, waits. Thirty seconds pass. Then the eleven footer bends hard in the middle, does a buggy-whip as the man backs up the surf, cranking, keeping the rod tip high. Two big flat fish, silvery at this distance, dance on the line—*double-trouble.* Two at a time, they put the bend on the man's rod and I see them flap when he unhooks, two, three-pounders, nice fish. Now and then, this Chinese man puts his rod in the surf spike and hikes over to a dark cliff wall where the tide rises. He digs and kicks and scrapes with his hands—some kind of bait over there. Then he retakes the rod, lands fish after fish—he could feed a multitude with what's in his cooler. How on earth will he carry the son of a bitch? I wish Renee here for this spectacle, and just like that I see her coming. My wife, who has somehow saved me from the worst–I know that much. Sometimes I'm shocked to see her, that her world is my world. Buoys exist.

I watch Renee Rockerson Harvell walk along the driftwood beach, barefoot in a white sun dress—pure-seeming as storks on the wing; Cape Codders for sailors' daughters—for whom I'd once written on a Carolina sand dune *I LOVE YOU!* in six foot tall letters composed entirely of horseshit from wild horses on the Outer Banks, ponies descended from Spaniard stallions. I'd gathered the manure one whole afternoon not far from the twisting Hatteras lighthouse while she drove in to the liquor store for more rum. "It's a bunch of shit," I said, and we split a gut, laughed our asses silly.

"Hey," Renee says, "You freezing your balls off?" She takes sleepy Lara, wraps her in a beach blanket. She's brought coffee, hands me a thermos and a cream cheese bagel.

"Look at this guy."

We sit side by side. The middle man lands a salmon—we see it hanging from his knee to the ground, rainbow colored as he carries it to the cooler. A Coho maybe, he's grinning ear to ear.

Renee says, "Dinner." She touches the back of my neck, kisses my cheek. "I'm taking little Miss for breakfast." She stands, cradles our growing girl, buries her face in my daughter's arms. "Love you," she says. "Love you, Daddy," Lara says, and I watch them walk away, the brutal and awesome Lookout Coast stretched out before them like a movie. When they stop and wave back, birds spiral overhead. A brace of cold salt air gets me in the face. I'm alive—I'm going to make it.

The Chinese man, the one who's in this Zen groove, smiles stands his rod in the surf spike and walks the wide beach to the cliff wall where he's gathered whatever he uses for bait.

When I walk up, he's bent over a mussel bed, kicking the fist-sized shells loose with his wader boot heel. Under the shells, where they've been attached to wet rock, a brown tentacle twitches and snakes and the Chinese man grabs this, pulls it out and slides it in his front pocket.

"Excuse me. What are you doing?"

The man—he's my size, thin and lean—turns on me and smiles, big white teeth, and he raises his brows in what I take to be a question. I hold my hands in front of my chest, like I'm gripping a rod while a fish jerks. "What are you *using?*"

His smile widens. He stands up straight, steps toward me. "*Sheep-ha,*" he says. "Sheep-ha!"

"Sheep ha?"

"*Sheep-ha!*" He sticks his fingers into the front pocket, heart side of his chest, pulls out a coiling worm, the size of his little finger, the length of his hand. Between thumb and index finger, the thing writhes right in front of my face. "Sheep-ha!" he shouts the third time with much conviction, as if understanding this gnarled worm is the key to the world. He shakes it in my face, raises his brows. He wants to make sure that I get it, that I seize what's happening this second. "Sheep-ha."

I say, "Sheep-ha" and nod.

He nods back, smiles. Then he walks away and leaves me the mussel bed, where I set immediately to kicking shells loose with river sandals, gathering up the tough-hided worms from the razor shelled mussel shoal, not at all an easy task though do-able, something I could learn and pass on. Two nights running, we eat fresh Ocean Perch for supper, the fillets fried golden the way I learned from Grandpa Stepwell, and I wish my pawnshop surf rod could only recall those fine bends: *Sheep-ha, blessed Sheep-ha. Our kind who art with Sheep-ha. Blessed be thy Sheep-ha, for thine is the kingdom, the power and the glory forever and ever, Amen.*

We spend a night on the water in Newport—where the mouth of the Elk River passes beneath a bridge of such splendor that I hesitate to speak it, lest the metaphor of bridges overtake me for all time. Concrete wonders—these Oregon Coast bridges, unbelievable. Lara and I walk the piers and docks and find a boat named Hydrotherapy, have the mate pull out a tuna fish and watch him dress it, the silver knife flashing as he papers the fillet, rolling the stone-eyed head into a trough where many others look up. "Sell these to a hog farm," he says, and I rock back on my shoes.

The fisherman pulls out makings and hand rolls a cigarette. He's talking to Lara, telling her about the whales out there in open water, how they sing a thousand miles underwater and breathe spouts tall as skyscrapers, how they look you in the eye and remember.

"Do sharks bite the whales?" Lara asks.

"No girl. No shark dare bite a whale. They're the queens and kings out there—from here to China."

He tosses me a can of beer from the fish cooler. Blood shines on the label and when I taste, I smell the fresh sweet scent of fish, and he can't know what this means to me, how it takes me to the Stepwells and Lake Ouachita, where voices carry over water in the dark before sun comes up, my mother's father tying the blood knot in ten-pound test, a devils toothpick dangling from a Pfleuger rod. Always about water, all waters lead home.

Driving south in the clear morning, we roll through these ancient sand dunes that seem like the moon, miles and miles of them, sand dunes drifting in the middle of a blue spruce forest. 101 drifts gently west again after Coos Bay, one state park after another, off the highway where every curve shocks you to the here and now. I've heard about a place that's hard to get to, read about it maybe in one of the *See Oregon* books Renee's rented from the library. This holy place for the natives where a lighthouse stands on a towering cliff, a Cape where an Irishman lived for thirty years in a fine house of blue spruce. He roused up every morning to operate the massive mirrors that shone off Cape Blanco, the furthest point west in the continental U.S., the end of the line, as far as she goes.

Cranberry bogs have sprung up now and we roll over a river named *Sixes*— who on earth names a river *Sixes*? Have I said that no one driving a vehicle in the state of Oregon is allowed to pump gas? A worker's thing—when jobs were scarce and the economy down, maybe about the time they decided to build all these state parks every three miles for four hundred miles of coast, it was decided that workers would be hired to pump gas at every station in the state, people would have jobs and the jobs would give them faith in themselves and they'd buy houses and take their kids to the dentist and make good salads and potatoes to eat with fresh fish. The world would make sense and sustain itself in Oregon—what a great, good place. The cranberry bogs are thick with berries near Port Orford, which I'll learn is one of the world's only open sea ports. Open water means no bay, just wide sea and these gigantic cranes to haul boats from the water each afternoon when they return from fishing, the holes filled with eels, albacore and salmon.

Cape Blanco State Park Road is off Highway 101, just past the Sixes River by a cranberry bog before the town of Port Orford. Renee's driving, about four in the afternoon, close enough to happy hour to want to be still, find a place to drink and eat and watch the sun set into the ocean. All along the coast, from Astoria down, we've scrambled for campsites in state parks crowded with noisy, good-hearted Oregonians out for the weekend, setting off fireworks and wolf-whistling. They're people like us. The young carry surfboards and wet suits in Jeeps, have forlorned looks on wise-looking faces; everyone seems full alert—great beauty makes you that way, it sharpens the consciousness. And I'm here to tell you, the Oregon Coast we've driven and camped is nothing if not the most physically beautiful piece of earth and sea that I've ever witnessed in my lifetime.

Today we're lucky. Renee's library book hints that a site at this Cape is a hard one to land with tent and camp stove. The sites are large, half-acre plots nearly, overrun with these rainbow butterflies and moths, with sweeping views out over the Pacific. Named Blanco by Vasco deGama, sailing north for the invisible northern passage to the Atlantic, the towering white cliffs are the furthest point west in the continental U.S., a point me and Renee make hay of during the drive down. Here is as far as you can get from Florida and Arkansas without jumping in the goddamn ocean and swimming. Campers come here to get away from the people and the fireworks and wolf whistles, to have the long and difficult beach to themselves, and they stay. Sixteen days is the max, but Renee's book says it's hard to get a spot, sometimes the place just books up and the site gates get shut. Whoever's in is in, and whoever's out is out.

But today we're lucky. Renee swings into the A-loop, where we immediately spot this big open site with a view west over the ocean just like the picture books, flat with big trees for tying drylines and airing sleeping bags. Three rabbits circle a table and grill grate, disappear into the thicket where an owl sounds over the waves and wind. We pay money to a benevolent couple of Michigan retirees, this peaceful look on their faces like they've been sipping wine from the Elysian Fields or smoking opium and all manner of things are well. Back at site 7 we break the truck down, set the tent and make camp. This is our tenth day out. We've stocked up on food and liquor and wine, and have long since put away the camera and video cam and given up on journals. I've yet to crack a book save the tour guide. Lara has one of those etch-a-sketch drawing pads, a magnetic pencil that writes on a grey screen where she makes whales and sea lions and her name. More than one time she's drawn the casket which she quickly erases when she sees me see. By six our makeshift home is put together, we've poured vodka tonics, and walk down the steep road through blue spruce, muddy and washed out in places, a hard road that opens onto three miles of isolated beach. Ancient driftwood—gigantic trees that lived on air that Julius Caesar breathed—has washed ashore in a maze that stretches clear north to Blanco, the great white arm of bluffs that forms the Cape.

We see the whales straight away.

Looking north and west, their spouts rise rhythmically and we can just make out the chiaroscuro bodies, a lighter shade of silver than the water. Lara walks the waterline where bones scatter in the wash; she picks up a frisbee-sized vertebrae and looks at us through it. "Peek-a-boo," she squeals.

A gray whale blows, maybe thirty yards out. We follow it or it follows us—I don't know. We walk abreast, the dark eyes on us. For a quarter mile we're silent. We look at the whale, the whale looks at us. I hear it breathe. Each time it rises Lara says, "Daddy?" and I'm hit square between the eyes with how it all works, this sudden *déja vu* like a veil's lifted; I swear to Jesus, like I've lived my whole life through and am now revisiting with a shot at changing the whole shebang. "Daddy?" Lara says, and the whale breathes—she sees us through.

Before dark, before we walk the steep muddy hill away from the beach and the gray whale whose eyes have followed us so carefully, the three of us sit on a tremendous log. Lara shakes her bones and Renee's still in dark glasses, her face like her mother's—Meg, way back east. "This is the right place," she says. "I'm glad we're here."

"Me, too," Lara says.

The air is wet and cold and the wind is northwest, the sun warping over the far curve of sea. I say, "Me three."

We find our way out in the dark. In sleep we roll near each other against the cold and dream. My grief-dreams follow patterns. The dead rise up, appear themselves and say it's okay and that they feel for you because of how you hurt. And sometimes they ask of you more than you're willing to commit—life for life, death for death, and sometimes they send out this ache, like a heart about to break. And sometimes they turn loose, and its up to you to find the way up the muddy hillside of the psyche, or not to find the way. There, we're all on bended knee, on boards lain over floors beside great bloated death, crying out *Oh can you hear me? Won't you please, please hear me?* Through the star window sewn into our tent roof, the sky spins. How many times have I lay in this dark and replayed my life—the many, many failures and missed chances? The deceits and cruelties and pettiness with which I've marked my time? In mirrors I see the trace of the man who snarled behind the glass. I see.

Daylight can be sensed long before it happens. And this is the dark time, real chill in the air, cold through my sleeping bag which is rated for zero, though I've heard those numbers are a lie. Every fourteen seconds, Cape Blanco's lighthouse strobes our tent, lighting my daughter's face where she lay breathing, the air rasping a little over big tonsils. She picked the wild blue flowers while Renee and I made dinner, formed a bouquet and told me to shut my eyes.

"Open, Daddio," she said.

And my eyes opened to this little girl with her hair blowing in the breeze off the ocean, her eyes wavering between smile and worry, a perfect mix of all my relations. She lifts the blue flowers up and wonders if I will take them.

"I love you," Lara said. "*Here.*"

A light rain falls on our tent roof. I hear the ocean and the ones breathing who love me, and the way these mix.

28.

Three days become five days, then seven, eight before we lose count and time becomes nameless, the way it must be for people after they accept being stranded at sea and begin to partake of the feast their senses offer. We wear no watches. Days ago Lara fed the last pages of an Arkansas Wildlife Calendar Issue to a beach fire, June's great blue heron piercing a sunfish with her bill burns into July's fiery hummingbird, the ruby throat drifting toward the water as the section titled *Sunrise and Sunset at Little Rock, Arkansas* ignites. That the road down the mountain to the surf is washed out and dangerous becomes a blessing—we have the place to ourselves most days, save the big fishing ships you see miles off, and the omnipresent whale spouts. We've come to recognize a few individuals, notably a mother with calf which Lara has named *Chucky* and *Chuquiña*. At two, maybe three miles, the stretch of ocean has a natural wall at either end. The southern boundary is a series of jagged cliffs, impassable for ships even at low tide when the beach widens. The northerly point is the Cape itself, towering up to a meadow with a panoramic view from the century old lighthouse with its saucy tour-guides—Kappa Deltas down for summer from the U of O in Eugene. From seventy, eighty miles at sea ships can sight light from the reflective lenses, the finest on earth, and I've wondered whether or not Cap ever rounded this piece of earth, where we've lost ourselves to the day by day routine of being. Approaching the beach and subsequent surf from the east is nearly impossible, the cliffs up to the Blanco plateau—and its Indian burial site—being sheer drop offs that not even rock climbers try. On the ocean side, polished rocks—house-sized islands alive with sea lions—jut from the sea. Obsidian-black points reflect water and sky, shine as sawteeth no ship nor boat will try. The rocks make a barrier between us and open sea, maybe a quarter mile out into the blue horizon that draws the eyes and is pleasing to look toward.

Moment to moment a whale blows, inside a rock's throw, you see them see you. I start talking to them when they're in close like that, when they look me in the eye and it's whatever time of day it is when I begin to speak to the whale that keeps swimming and sounding beyond the first breaker. Her calf is in tow, blowing air columns in big shiny bursts that whish upward and are so real that it seems my heart will break. The names of the days have gone away. I'm just a man on a fingernail of earth with a woman and a child. We've come clear across a continent, I don't know why. I face the whale on a day that I don't know a name for—open up and begin to tell, to make the words that come before anything. Open up, speak, make the words.

Maybe that's how it all starts, on the beach, this beach, the gulls screaming over my head and the clouds. It's cold and I wear fleece, my bare feet in the sand, Lara and Renee somersaulting down the magnificent fine-sand mountain that centuries have blown up against the Cape. They climb together to the top, a real struggle up a hundred yards of steep pitch, sand to their calves, then they stand on top, two, three hundred feet up there and catch their breaths. Lara points seaward—her mother brings a hand to her eyes—a salute for whale-seeing, Cape Codders for sailors' daughters. Then they hold hands and leap forward, whoop fiercely and come somersaulting down.

We've discovered a dead sea lion just downwind. As big as a horse, the mouth grins skyward. The three of us laid flowers on its sunken head and made a prayer for the dead and the living—for everything about to fall. How to pinpoint when one becomes a man who prays? Some mighty transition must occur, shouldn't it, before a man who never prays says a prayer, laces his daughter's blue wild flowers into the stinking fur of a bloated sea lion? When the wind is right, the smell overpowers. To begin to pray over such a thing, swum in to die or killed at sea, why should it matter? Yesterday, or the day before or the day before, I took my daughter's hand in one hand and my wife's in the other, and we stood over a dead sea lion and prayed and offered flowers for the journey home. Behind me now, up on the high sand mountain, Lara and Renee are rolling down and down and down beyond the ancient driftwood that criss-crosses this sliver of earth with no entrance save ours. And this whale, a gray maybe, or a humpback—what do

I know about whales?—keeps swimming inside a stone's throw, just out behind the first breaker. I could surfcast a goddamn plug straight out to its face, snag a treble hook and hello Jesus, but instead I start talking. Nobody can hear me, save this gray whale that's maybe a humpback; she looks me through with her soulful eye then disappears only to rise again, swimming the other way, pacing the shallows outside the first breaker. Why? I can't know why. The Irishman who operated the lighthouse for thirty years is buried up on the hill, not far from the house he built with his sons and wife, all long dead. All that time in this wind-beaten desolation, the company of whales and sea lion, screaming birds and the endless suppers of fish and garden greens, wild mushrooms from the forest floor. Out here in true wilderness, barn building with timbers from wrecked ships, the gathered eggs from white cliffsides. The wife had missed her home back in Ireland, and when he died, this thirty-year lighthouse operator, she'd left him here, set his stone on the hill alcove facing Ireland. She'd walked away from her husband's grave and gone by ship across the Atlantic and never come back, even though the sons and daughters are buried at their father's feet.

I have not cried since the first morning, not for Mama and not for me. Girlish voices sing-song behind me. The ocean heaves and the sky's laced with east-moving stratocumuli and cirrus. The new moon's out, the old moon in its arms. The gray tacks not forty yards out. In the corner of my eye, Lara and Renee drag driftwood into a heap, the summer sun straight over our heads, the day full ahead. We're at the edge of a new world—this much seems true—dragging the freight of our lifetimes. The wind is right this second and I smell the sea lion, a big cow, four-hundred pounds maybe, rotting up beyond the sand mountain. Lara and Renee are fashioning the driftwood into a makeshift shelter. The smell is unmistakable, what happens to flesh and blood. I understand the association of flowers and death, how the two go hand in hand, through where prayer originates is a great mystery. I don't know when I fell in love with my mother. Maybe the body remembers with intense nostalgia its first home, so our powerful attraction to see and swim in oceans, to gather fishes and shells and weeds offered up, in dangerous waters. The undertow of our dreams drowns us. From those waters came our kind. Sea water is suitable, so I've read, for pumping into a human's veins in place of blood, should none be on hand. Love of water is love of self—the trail our tears make, ancient springs where all our initials are carved and sweet water flows between fissures in the walls of time: *water of life, water of death.*

A mountain of sand has blown up against one sheer cliff just to the south of the white cape. Coarse, the sand is the color of the stone though it holds heat and can be climbed to the summit way up high. Renee and Lara are down now, building a driftwood shelter. I stand up and begin the climb, my own voice in my ears. Up where they've gone before me. I could surfcast a goddamn plug straight out to its face, the gray swimming within a hard stone's throw, but instead I'm talking, my voice, my own voice. Breath burns in my chest. I'm climbing as fast as I can, shouting *Daddy* through the sheet rock. Words held for so long now they ignite. From the top of the sand mountain, out into this vast sea and sky—the very end of the line: don't *hurt* her. Don't *hurt* her. Daddy, don't *hurt* her. *Please. Stop fucking hurting her.*

All those long days thinking in that truck, forging your hours into the logbooks between states, ten tons of slaughter turkeys in tow, you've miscalculated. Had you counted on me being drunk? The Christmas Day I was born, me and Mama took each other to the threshold, my eyes shut, hers full open, the hemorrhaging where I drowned for a time, *o dark river.* On the ferry of my mother's blood, we took each other to the stone world where I drowned in her as she does in me. All these years, *help me Joey, he's killing me*—the words twisting and turning in my dreams. Are you listening? Can you hear me? Through the CB chatter, do you recognize my voice? See how I come for you hidden in her veils? *I call your bluff. Trucks don't roll uphill, O.W. They never goddamn will.*

From on top of the sand mountain, my wife and daughter are small, the tiny beach fire, a ribbon of smoke. Renee has fashioned timbers across two ancient trees and built walls on three sides and a flat ceiling. The door faces west, open ocean where the whales are swimming just beyond the first breaker. Lara's wild flowers are laced into the sea lion's fur. I watch this world from the furthest point west in my country, my back to the white cliffs where the sand mountain leans. The whales swim close enough for us to see their eyes and they ours—see my wife and daughter hauling gear into the makeshift house where a beach fire now burns before the open door. Renee shakes out an Indian blanket from our backpack, drags it inside where I imagine her forming the four corners into the rough walls, making the place fit for us to lay down and rest. Sun falls gleaming on the water for miles and miles. The air I breathe is chill and salty.

Down in front of our driftwood home, Lara warms her hands, palms open to the beach fire flames. All the things that will happen in her lifetime begin from here, the bonehouse her mother makes, stretching the blue tarp across the door's open mouth. Navajoes believe there's great good luck in blue doors, good medicine. This second the door folds upward. Renee steps out again and sees me see her. She smiles, then disappears into the shelter. The ocean seems blank, a slate, a breath about to happen. In front of the lean-to, just beyond the flames, Lara tromps a crude heart, ten-feet tall, into the sand, turns and flashes a smile up over her shoulder. From where I stand, she looks like a younger version of Mama, like my mother as a girl with the wind in her hair. In the last moment, just before the heart closes, she holds out both hands for balance. My daugher's feet lift and fall gently over the last three steps. Much caution, the business of hearts. Across the gulf between us, her concentration is unmistakable. Four years old, she believes she knows. She flashes one last smile—and it's done.

A day will come when I go home to open my mother's room. Through a floral blouse, I will breathe her and in the seams of her letters see the word again and again and again. *Love*, the one buoy, what remains when the world quiets and the crude heart is tromped.

One day soon, I'll lay Stepwell blocks around her grave, light sage on a medicine wheel and the smoke will whirl upward through the hickories. Blackberry will bloom down the barbed wire fence and the cut turf will mend. Copperheads will taste the air with dark tongues and the land will be furious with life.

So I let myself go, free for the moment from this earth's ties. I tumble and roll—earth, air, sky then water—until the fall is complete. Then I make my way past Lara's heart to the makeshift home, lift the bright blue door and go inside.

About the Author

Michael Gills' first collection of short fiction, *Why I Lie*, was published by U. of Nevada Press/2002. It won a Utah Book Prize, was a finalist for the Arkansas' Porter Prize and was chosen as a top literary debut by *The Southern Review*. A second collecion, *The Death of Bonnie and Clyde*, will be out from Texas Review Press in October 2011, the title story of which won Southern Humanities Review's Hoepfner Prize for the best story published there in 2010. A third collection of stories, *Eternally Yours*, is currently on the market. Gills has published more than forty short stories, received 25 Pushcart nominations, and held the Randall Jarrell Fellowship at the University of North Carolina. He holds additional degrees from the University of Arkansas and the University of Utah where he earned the Ph.D. His fiction has appeared or is forthcoming in *New Madrid*, *Boulevard*, *The Texas Review*, *The Gettysburg Review*, *The Greensboro Review*, *Shenandoah*, *Quarterly West*, *The Oxford American*, *Wasatch Journal*, *Salt Hill*, *Lynx Eye*, *Moon City Review*, *The Chattahoochee Review*, *Southern Humanities Review*, *McSweeney's*, *Verb*, *New York Stories*, *New Stories From The South* and elsewhere. A Utah Established Artist grant recipient, Gills is currently Associate Professor/Lecturer of writing and core faculty for the Honors College at the University of Utah. *Go Love* is his first novel.

www.ingramcontent.com/pod-product-compliance
Lightning Source LLC
Chambersburg PA
CBHW020614250626
47154CB00004B/1510